Arlene Schindler

The Last Place She'd Look

This book is a work of fiction. The names, characters and incidents are products of the writer's imagination, or are used fictitiously. Any resemblance to persons living or dead, events, or locales is purely coincidental.

No part of this book may be reproduced, or stored in a retrieval system, or transmitted in any form or by any means, electronic, mechanical, photocopying, recording, or otherwise, without express written permission of the author.

Copyright © 2013 by Arlene Schindler

All rights reserved.

ISBN: 13 978-0615762876

Cover design by Scarlett Rugers
www.scarlettrugers.com

Book design: Jackie Hoffman Chin

Back cover photograph: Dennis Apergis

www.ArleneSchindler.com

First Edition

2013 ExtravaGonzo Publishing

Acknowledgements:

A tremendous debt of gratitude to the many who helped make The Last Place She'd Look a reality, especially the following people for many and varied reasons:

Arlene Phalon Baldassari, Jackie Hoffman Chin, Terry Delsing, Kathleen Fairweather, Julie Falen, Lyn Holley, Debbie Kasper, Bob Keenan, Catherine Leach, Meg Livesey, Janet Lombardi, Mary McGrath, Leslie Parsons, Linda Schwab, Dan Staroff.

Thank you to my best girls for being funny, kind, constructively creative and supportive.

Special thanks to Elaine Silver, for her guidance, support, and cheerleading that helped me arrive at the finish line.

Contents
☙☙☙

Ack the Hack 1

Will Having a Relationship Make Me OK?
  OR Will Being OK Get Me a Relationship? 17

Yoga Geezer 27

Face the Music 39

Soakin' It Up 52

Out Night Girls 64

Back In the Game 73

My Late Date 80

Beauty By the Lb. 84

Divas Of the Dungeon 88

Theater Games 95

Cancer Victors and Their Friends 108

Party Faces 113

Brunchin' Babes 118

Lavender Visions 126

The Ambivi-sexual 138

Color My World 146

Crashing Waves 153

What Now? 167

Are You Bisexual? 189

Contents
☙ ☙ ☙

Hot Flash 198

Light My Fire 204

Are You In a Dangerous Relationship? 214

Stick Shift 220

School Daze? 228

Mouseburger No More 234

Real Love? Real Estate 243

Self-Pleasure Shopping 249

COOL: The Future? 254

Love Means Never Having to Say You're Sorry 261

Help Me to Help Myself And Help You Too 278

Big Fat Check 283

Dream On…It Takes Two 290

Little Pink House 303

1. Ack the Hack
꽃꽃꽃

As his muscular leg swung off the sleek mountain bike he was riding, I was excited to see that this guy had a hot body. At first glance my date looked sexy and promising.

I wanted to believe this blind date would be my last first date. The next week I turned 50. After a half century I wanted to stop the "Hello, my name is…" merry-go-round and actually relate to someone for a significant period of time.

But I should know better. I'm Sara, and my friends think I'm a dateaholic, just because in the past few years I've had 340 first dates. Please note that in my case dateaholism has <u>not</u> meant that I am a sex addict as evidenced by the fact that none of these dates led to sex, most not even a kiss, (much to my chagrin and disappointment). Every addict hits bottom at some point, and 341 was it for me. So let me tell you about my last first date. Let me also tell you about my subsequent surprising journey to recovery (and lots of sex — thank goodness!).

It was 10 a.m. on a Saturday, early summer. Sitting at an outdoor table at Swingers, a diner/café in a trendy area of Los Angeles, I was eager to meet my blind date from *match.com*: Karl Acker, an English professor at Occidental College who taught creative writing to freshmen. We'd seen each other's photos on line, so while locking his bike to a parking meter, he blurted breathlessly before he even sat down. "I bike every day and swim five times a week."

"Wow," I said, smiling, admiring his torso, and thinking about my lazy self, "I wash the dishes every day and take the garbage out about five times a week."

"What do you do to keep in shape?" he asked, now sitting facing me, purposefully eyeing me up and down.

"I take the stairs instead of elevators," I joked. He looked disappointed. "And," I lied, "I do yoga a few times a week."

"So you're bendy and flexible?" he said, perking up, hoping this was a glimpse of scenarios to come. "I've been up since 5:30 this morning. I've already eaten. Just a chai latte for me."

Self-conscious on a first date, concerned about appearing ladylike, and not wanting to be viewed as a voracious behemoth, I ordered tea and a small bowl of fruit.

"What do you do when you're not biking and swimming?" I asked, trying to find an activity that I could participate in — something quasi-sedentary like movies, theater, or slow walks through museums.

"I teach. I enjoy my students. Young minds are so fertile, full of ideas. And I'm writing a novel."

Now I was intrigued. "What's it about?"

"The Vietnam War, how life has been for my buddies."

"They were in 'Nam?"

"Conscientious objectors," he declared proudly. Our eyes met. His were a piercing blue, like ocean waves: relaxing, peaceful, mesmerizing. Looking closely at him, I realized his face seemed twice the age of his body; it was fascinatingly strange.

"And you?" he asked, reaching for my hand. It felt as though he was forcing a connection, but I was willing to play along.

"I've never been to Vietnam," I said, lightly.

"What do you do?"

"I write articles for self-help magazines — relationships, fashion tips, how to get the most out of your IRA. You know, psycho-babble for women's publications — but somebody's got to do it."

"I wrote pulp fiction before I started teaching," he replied.

"What about the 'Nam novel?"

"I've been writing it since I've been teaching, 10 years," he said, laughing. Then there was silence. I sipped my tea, thinking about what to ask next. I felt his eyes exploring my body, trying to X-ray through my denim jacket to my slight shoulders and small breasts. He looked at his watch. "I've got to meet my daughter. She's 17. I hope you'll let me call you."

"Karl, I think that would be nice," I said demurely, like a shy ingénue in a Henry James novel. We both stood up and walked the few steps to his bike.

"Call me Ack. That's what my friends call me," he said self-assuredly. He pulled on my lapel with one hand as he touched my chin with the other and leaned into me for a sweet kiss, but I didn't feel much chemistry. I dejectedly walked the four blocks home to my apartment, expecting to never hear from him again.

Three days later, Ack called and invited me to his house for dinner, our second date. He was geographically desirable because he lived a mere mile away from me. Lack of chemistry aside, he offered a hot meal and male attention — two things I was starving for.

I drove to his place around sunset, a tiny guesthouse on the side of someone else's property. He and his aging Irish setter greeted me. Ack was barefoot, looking sexy in his well-worn jeans, holding a wooden spoon. "Taste this," he commanded, moving the spoon to my mouth before I could say hello. "It needs something."

I tasted the spaghetti sauce. "Oregano and garlic."

"Yes!" Snapping his fingers with the other hand, he gave me a swift peck on the cheek before ushering me straight into the kitchen. "My creation lives! Follow me."

In the kitchen, he stirred the simmering pot of sauce, then lowered the flame. "You need wine, lots of wine," he said, grinning, pouring from a giant jug of cheap Chianti into two mismatched wine glasses. Giving me one, he raised his. "To tonight."

We clinked glasses and sipped. In his kitchen, Ack was genial, boyish, and goofy — he was growing on me. I looked around the crowded, messy kitchen and poked my head into the living room and his office. All were cluttered with thrift store furniture. At mid-life, Ack's home was not the abode of a thriving college professor; it resembled the studio of a struggling student. In spite of his rundown digs, there was a youthful, endearing charm here too.

Dinner was served on mismatched plates with paper napkins and silverware that looked like it had been stolen from a school cafeteria. The spaghetti was from a box that was still poking out of the garbage pail, the sauce from a jar that was sitting beside the sink. I got the definite impression that he chose to make dinner because he couldn't afford to take me out.

We ate at a rickety kitchen table. Shortly after I sat down, he got up again to reposition the matchbook jammed under one of the table legs. Then he smiled at me. "More wine…you need more wine. Drink up."

My fork forged into the mound of spaghetti and sauce on my plate. Although enthusiastic, presentation was not his forte. The strands of spaghetti were so long, I worked to twirl the pasta onto my fork gracefully. That was impossible. The only way to eat this meal was to stab a mound of spaghetti, shove it into my mouth, and bite away. Eating was work. It tasted flavorless. But I was hungry for the companionship of a handsome, intelligent man.

"Do you cook a lot?" I tried to inject dialogue into the spaghetti challenge.

"I have to feed my teen-aged daughter. She's a vegetarian."

"Where is she now?"

"Sleeping over at a girlfriend's house. She lives with me full-time."

"What about her mother?"

"A flower child who found other things to do. She's living on a commune in Washington," he explained, filling my glass again.

"Are we having a wine-drinking contest?" I asked.

"I just want to make sure you're having a good time."

"This meal is very…filling," I replied, putting my fork down.

"No dessert unless you finish this glass of wine," Ack insisted.

"I don't think I'll have room for dessert." I rubbed my stomach and sneakily unbuttoned the top button of my jeans.

"I made a key lime pie in a graham cracker crust. You'll find room," he insisted, quickly clearing the table, tossing the dishes in the sink with the leftover food and forks. "Let's take our wine and go to the living room," he continued, ushering me to the main clutter-ateria of his home. The coffee table was brimming with hardcover books, each with a bookmark. There was a wooden rocking chair near a far window. Strewn with mounds of reading matter, scattered mail, and record albums, no rugs on the worn wooden floors, this room was eclectic but less than inviting.

"Sit on the couch," he urged, gently stroking my shoulder after putting the wine glasses on the table in between the piles of books.

"Looks like you read a lot," I offered.

"These are books my friends wrote. I'm waiting for mine to be published."

"When's it coming out?"

"It's not finished yet. I'm still writing, rewriting…soon," he said, reflecting. "Now you, you write…? Don't tell me…"

"Self-help for magazines," So thrilled that a man had finally shown some interest in me, I ignored the fact that he hadn't remembered our first conversation.

"I don't read self-help. I try to discourage my daughter, too, but I guess it's a living, right?" He stroked my back and nuzzled my shoulder, then kissed my neck, working his way feverishly, faux passionately, to my mouth.

One moment we were sitting on the couch discussing writing, the next, Ack had his tongue down my throat, playing a clumsy boy's game of tonsil hockey. Ten seconds later, he was using his sexy, athletic shoulders to push me down onto the couch so he could climb on top of me — without missing one second of tongue-probing. Nimble, then more forcefully, he jutted his pelvis against mine, spastically banging his crotch into me again and again. As he hardened, each thrust became more unpleasant. His mouth never paused in its exploration of mine, as if the centrifugal force of the earth in the solar system would be devastated if he stopped.

I was not aroused — or amused. I tried to remember the last time I'd been touched…was it only two years ago? It felt like forever. That painful realization kept me there, in spite of the aggressive, oppressive foreplay. I wished I had the emotional strength to push him off of me. Finally, I broke free of the Tupperware-hermetic lip lock to gasp for air — only to have Ack rally with some swift yoga move. He shimmied his head past mine as he swerved his torso up my body. His head swayed, cobra-like, off the arm of the well-worn couch, and his chest was inches from my forehead.

Astonished by his animated pushiness, this awkward ballet of adolescent-style seduction didn't captivate me, but I did feel a bit captive. I kept thinking — a man was finally touching me! — so I stayed put. Maybe this would get better. If nothing else, our desperation was compatible. I wanted to give him a chance.

Meanwhile, Ack's erection was moving, slithering up my body like a denim-armored snake — now wriggling between my breasts. He twisted to the side and let out a guttural sigh as he softly maneuvered his hardness into a comfortable spot — for him.

I winced as his belt buckle jammed into my armpit. Ack twisted again, lifting up, whipping the entire belt out of its loops with one yank and whoosh. Then, no surprise, he unbuttoned and unzipped his jeans. With that same hand, he released his penis from his pants, head bobbing through the zipper, and pressed it against me like a puppy in a pet shop window, eager for attention with the hope of being taken home and cuddled. This same hand five seconds later found my hand and placed it on the aforementioned member. He then moved my hand to show me the way he liked to be stroked. He was, after all, a teacher by profession. Had students been in this same position, as part of their course of study — or maybe for extra credit? If his conquests were a steady diet of post-adolescents, it would explain his seduction style, or lack thereof.

My behind was now slowly sliding into the space between the couch cushions, sort of a tush-and-sofa sandwich. As I lay there, I heard, *"Helplessly hoping his harlequin hovers nearby ..."* a soft, gentle Crosby, Stills and Nash tune on the CD player. No doubt Ack had been using the same musical selection for seductions since his youth, when the album was a record on his turntable. I recalled a slogan of the Woodstock generation, also on this same album: *"Love the one you're with."*

Ack writhed and twisted again, until his erection now bobbed near my chin. I knew where he wanted it to go. I turned my head in the opposite direction, non-compliant. This wasn't desire for me, nor was it any pleasure. It was just a cocksman using my body to get himself off. Half of me wanted to bolt up and run out...but the other half was woozy and conflicted.

Ack twisted my neck, forcing my mouth to face and greet his cock. This move of his was neither boyish nor pleasant. As the tip of his penis grazed my lips, my inner voice prompted, *"Bite it. That'll teach him."* Unfortunately, the only lesson learned was by me — Chianti and pasta form a lethal, lethargic combination.

My neck wrenched with a loud and audible crack, like a nut being shelled.

"Are you all right? You're not comfortable here, are you?"

I couldn't speak with his erect penis in my mouth, so I mumbled, like a mute. He jumped up and off of me, almost looking me in the eye. "Let's get more comfortable. Let's go upstairs." He grabbed my arm and with one yank, pulled me out of the wedge between the couch cushions, up on my feet, half-floating, half-standing.

Stymied by his speed, too foggy and dazed to think quickly of an excuse not to go up the stairs, the next thing I knew, I was at the doorway of his bedroom. He turned on a small reading light on the shabby night table. The full-size bed had worn, almost-white bed sheets — not crisp, not clean, like a college boy's dorm room. There were sweat socks lurking near the windowsill.

Ack smirked, pleased he'd dragged his prey into his lair. He touched my chin with his fingertips, grazing my mouth with his lips. Seconds later, his awkwardly orchestrated dance of seduction continued. He removed his T-shirt, revealing perfectly sculpted and tan biceps, triceps, and a taut midsection. The only giveaway that he wasn't 25 was the colony of white hair populating his chest. More pleased with himself by the minute, Ack displayed the coy style of a stripper, slyly slithering his jeans to the floor, revealing the well-defined calves, thighs, and buns of a daily mountain biker.

Ack in his naked glory was confident he had the hottest, hardest body of any 55-year-old in town. In better shape than even most movie stars, he stood proud, as if I should fall at his feet and fawn at his perfection.

"This is me," he said, proudly, lifting his arms into a pose like a circus artist after he's performed on the high wire, ready to take a bow. I was annoyed by his arrogance, which was escalating to bitch-slapping proportions. I swayed, fully clothed, alien to his self-admiration. His naked reveal had a "ta-da" at the end of it that sickened me; his appreciation for his own physical beauty was pungently distasteful.

I focused on the moment. Even though he was an arrogant jerk, he did have an Adonis physique. The promise of something good still existed for my sex-starved self. He'd taken me into his home, his bedroom, wined and dined me (sort of). I was primed.

"Now you," he said, eager for a provocative performance. He gestured for me to remove my clothes. First my shirt, then pants, bra, finally panties. I was quick and unromantic. The moment felt like a fire drill of nakedness.

Nude and imperfect, I anxiously wished my dimply, cellulite-ridden thighs were not on display. As he scrutinized my body, his smile faded, replaced with a polite frown. I sensed he'd hoped my form would rival his in youthful tone and beauty. No such luck for either of us.

Ack ushered me to the bed. He climbed in, too, and covered me with the white sheet. At first, I thought this cozy gesture was for my comfort. He reclined, putting his head on the pillow, hands behind his head, in charge, in his own bed, taking a deep breath, then another. My head had just hit the pillow next to his. I heard him sigh.

"You know, I really should walk my dog right now," he suddenly uttered matter-of-factly. He climbed over me and got out of bed. He walked to the corner of the room, where just moments before he'd shed his jeans and shirt. Ever the minute man, he was dressed again. "Relax. I'll be right back," he said, exiting like a talk show host encouraging you to watch the commercials.

I lay in this almost-stranger's bed — alone. Now he had to walk his dog? This guy's a nut. Let's hope he fucks like a 25-year-old — and doesn't just think he does. He acts like he's an award-winner for stud puppet theater. What if I'm not turned on? He won't know or care. He'll dive into me like I was just another lap pool.

I turned on my side. The mattress and pillows were uncomfortable; the worn sheets were rough on my skin. I heard the sound of his dog scampering back into the house, the click as the leash was removed, a chain clattering on the wooden floors. Ack's footsteps creaked up the uncarpeted stairs. Entering the room without looking at me, he said robotically, "I can't do this…tonight. I have to get up early in the morning. I forgot I promised to help someone from work move. You'll have to go."

Suddenly, cold sober, I said to myself, "What you really mean is, 'I lost my appetite to fuck you because your body wasn't as trophy-worthy as mine.'" But instead, what came out was, "You don't even want me to sleep here? To cuddle?" I couldn't believe what I'd said. Was I testing the waters for future encounters? With this schmuck? Was I that desperate?

He turned, gathered my clothes in a ball, and dropped them on the bed, then, spinning on his heel, he left the room, speeding into the bathroom, and closed the door. When I was his daughter's age, I modeled in local fashion shows. Now, I just lay there, my self-esteem as crumpled as my clothes.

The air was icy with dysfunctional disappointment as I dressed. Just as I put my shoes on, I heard the toilet flush. I wondered if he'd jerked off.

He walked me to my car with all the courtesy of a recruiter ending the interview where you both know you didn't get the job. His lips grazed my forehead with a parental, dismissive kiss.

My car door closed. I drove away. By the first traffic light, my heart was racing, blood boiling. Was I rejected the moment he saw me naked? Was he too repulsed by my body to even have a one-night stand? Ack was humping on the couch like his life depended on getting laid. Then he deemed me unworthy to worship at the Ack-altar of testosterone.

This was more of a violation than an attempted rape. He chewed and spit out his desire for me like a stale piece of bubble gum now relegated to a life on pavement until it snuck onto someone's shoe. He didn't think my body was worthy of his, Spartacus warrior asshole. Judgmental, cruel bastard.

2. Will Having a Relationship Make Me OK? OR Will Being OK Get Me a Relationship?
🐚🐚🐚

How repulsed does a man have to be to throw a naked woman out of his bed without fucking her? The next morning, feeling every sense of self-worth slipping away, I replayed that thought in my mind a dozen times. I didn't want to believe Ack could be so cruel or that I could feel so rejected.

I'd sliced and diced my self-esteem by subjecting myself to too many blind dates, about a third of which turned into second dates, and few of which ever led to third dates, much less lasting relationships. None led to sex. This bewildered me. I approached each date with peppy optimism, freshly washed hair, glossed lips, and as much hope as I could muster. Yet I kept getting things wrong over and over…over 340 times, to be exact. I bit my nails and stewed with regret, disappointment, and defeat — wondering why I hadn't found anybody.

Why did I put myself into such unsatisfying situations? I should know better. I hoped for the best, anticipated the worst, wore sexy panties, and prayed that each date I was with THE right person.

These feelings were compounded by the fact that my 50th birthday was looming, lurking with foreboding like the soundtrack from the film *Jaws*. Was I the shark trying to envelop my prey? Or was I the one-piece bathing-suited swimmer praying that some Speedo-clad Adonis would find, flirt, and invite me to his beach house? In reality I saw myself as a single, middle-life, peri-menopausal woman. (I said "middle-life" because if I called myself middle-aged, it felt so much older, closer to elderly. At 50, how many people did I know who were 100? Who were their partners, and how old were they?) Pushing 50, eager for a date, searching for a mate is difficult — and depressing — a lot like shopping for a gift on Christmas Eve; everything I saw was either picked over or highly irregular. That's how I felt about the supply of men who would even look at me.

Once upon a time, I was married. It was in the Jurassic era, or so it seemed. Bringing up my married years was as relevant to any conversation as my SAT scores. It wasn't a good marriage or a long marriage — yet it was a life-defining moment. So I still dragged it around like a heavy suitcase with a broken handle. Divorced before 30, I'd spent most of my life since then feeling overlooked and alone, in spite of the winning qualities my friends told me I had.

Sure, I'd had a six-month relationship probably every three to five years over the past two decades. No, make that one blip of a person every five to seven years. But for the most part, I was alone.

Sometimes I'd regale friends with my dating mishaps, mainly if my experiences were so absurd that I didn't feel chipped at or eaten away. For example, many people have told me about first dates where the person they'd met was really someone 20 years older or 100 pounds heavier than their photo. One date I had was both. His reason for meeting me was that he was hoping that dating a writer would be easier and cheaper than taking a writing class. If he found me attractive, as he said, "Maybe I'll give you a crack at writing my memoir. I was a tennis pro (Yeah, I thought, about 18 years and 85 pounds ago). Ya know, I've dated women prettier and sexier than you. But with you I might actually learn something. So I'd give you a tumble. Whaddya say?"

There was another guy who spoke with me on the phone, three separate occasions for two hours each time, captivated by my witty patter. He told me he couldn't wait to meet me. I was eager about this one, too. I thought we had rapport. I met him outside a restaurant on a Tuesday night. He took one look at me, then horrified, looked down and away, as if the sight of me was so repulsive, he was checking to see if he'd puked on his own shoes. What did he think a mid-life woman looked like? Surely he'd seen my photos. No first date ever made me feel more rejected or uglier in an instant. Is it any wonder I can't remember his name?

My sadomasicism continued when we entered the dimly lit restaurant. He told the maître d' we'd sit at the bar, not staying for dinner, just drinks and appetizers. He was still with me, doing me a favor, but didn't think I rated a table. He balked at a nine dollar bowl of soup, ordered it anyway, and proceeded to slurp it like my grandpa when he didn't have his dentures in. During the slurping my date never looked at me.

Finally, as he spooned the last slurp, my self-esteem surfaced, explaining, "I just developed this really bad headache. Maybe we should try this another time."

"Yeah, me too," he said. Quickly eyeing our waiter, he requested the check and asked me to pay for my wine. I saw it as a small price to pay to end the agony.

Finally, back in my car, I felt comforted by the familiar clicking sound of my seat belt and the car engine revving. The next thing I heard were my own sobs as I cried, tears blurring my view as I drove all the way home to my momentarily tidy (but empty of another breathing soul) apartment.

I could make these dates sound funny, but the bigger question was, why did I subject myself to these humiliating encounters? Could I have behaved any differently and created another, more positive outcome? Was my stink of desperation perfume that repellent? Did I want too much? Did I not give enough of myself?

Sick of being the token single at coupled dinner parties, or the sympathy guest at Thanksgiving dinner, I dreaded every heartbreaking holiday season, thinking, "Who will invite me to spend the holidays with them? How will I hide my empty-hearted sadness when I get there?" I'd probably die of a broken heart, or be ignored and wither away like an abandoned house plant. I felt as lost as a cow without a cowbell...only cows had thinner thighs. Cows knew how to graze in the grass on a sunny day and appreciate the moment. I could take lessons…move to a farm. Maybe a fat farm.

I lost 50 pounds the last year of college, anxious about finding a job in the working world. My reward was a trip to the hairdresser who transformed my limp, mousy brown locks into flattering tresses with highlights and lowlights in dark blonde tones. That's been my color ever since — high-maintenance and high-priced. I charged it when I was broke.

I'm probably still paying off hair appointments from three years ago on my never-decreasing credit card balance.

Did any of this make me feel pretty? In the dating world a new hairdo always made me feel courageous and spunky, ready to welcome a warm smile offering kind words. Yet sometimes I wondered if I was just repainting an old barn, filled with dusty, anguished junk, eager to disguise it as glowing vintage artifacts. For the most part, whenever I took my lonely self on over 300 dates with the goal of not being alone in the future, I found myself sitting face-to-face with another breathing being, yet I was soul-less. So how could I have appeared attractive to them if I was invisible to myself? Over the years, as I grew confident, receptive, and welcoming, I thought the outcome of first dates that never led anywhere would change. As I became less invisible to myself, I believed my outcome would evolve; I'd at least have a two-week euphoric roller coaster of a romance that would be cast aside like Christmas morning's favorite toy. That would be an improvement over date after date ending with a forced smile, rigid hand shake, and the robotic mouthing of, "Nice to meet you."

Then I hit my 40s. Ouch. I'd become strong, self-affirming, and grounded. Finally present for my meet and greets, the tables had turned. The youth boat had sailed, leaving me imperceptible to the opposite sex. As much as I tried to have hope in my heart, I felt increasingly invisible as a desirable woman in the company of available, age-appropriate men. (Age-appropriate men — now that's an oxymoron. A middle-aged man who has never been married is a man-child. Living in Los Angeles, man-children are as plentiful as fake boobs.) They were self-absorbed, bitter about their pasts, eager for a companion who wouldn't make them "think too much." Most men seemed to want someone young enough to give them children (whether they wanted kids or not). Gazing at men's lined, saggy faces, receding hairlines, and expanding bellies, I thought the male population hovering around my age seemed dull and lifeless.

What did men see when they looked at me? Many times when our eyes met for the first time, I sensed they were saying, "Light me up, right now. Show me the magic of your hot, sexy love." Who can live up to that one-minute do-or-die first impression? Comedian Bill Maher said, *"There comes a time when women should just forget about men. It's called menopause."* Was this happening to me? Having spent most of my life as a celibate heterosexual, this was a tough concept to embrace. Then I thought, "Was I an unsuccessful heterosexual?" I'd been climbing the penis tree for so long, and the results were seldom worth the hike. If I was as wonderful, funny, and interesting as most friends said I was, then why was finding a relationship so difficult?

I called Julia, my personal goddess of self-esteem. She said, *"Hello"* before I heard her drop the phone, pick it up, drop it again, and finally slur, "Hello, who is this?"

"Are you hung over?" I whispered.

"Sara? What if I am?" I heard Julia strike a match, no doubt her first cigarette of the day.

"I am, too," I nervously laughed.

"Good for you." I heard her puffing, waking up. "Get any?"

"I could say 'close but no cigar', but the guy took one look at my body and threw me out of his house," I told Julia as I poured a sobering cup of coffee.

"If he couldn't see your beauty, then you're better off. He's a jerk, so on to the next." She puffed again and asked, "This ignoramus was a homeowner?"

"No, he lives in a rented dump…too broke for a decent bottle of wine."

"Don't spend another minute thinking about him. Get yourself to a yoga class, have a hot bath, and move on."

"Julia, want to go to yoga with me?"

"I'd love to, dear, but only if we can hit a noon class. Later today I have a guy coming over that I found on Craigslist. I've also seen him on Adult Friend Finders. Anyway, he'll be here to scrub my kitchen floors on his hands and knees while I spank him. Then he'll vacuum nude and service my sexual needs."

"Sounds like a full afternoon," I replied enviously.

"It's better than hiring a housekeeper — and there's a bonus! By sunset tonight, everything in my house will sparkle, including me," said Julia. "Check back in a few days. We'll go out. Remember what Eleanor Roosevelt said, 'No one can make you feel inferior without your consent.' Can you imagine her body? And you know, she had a girlfriend! Just food for thought, Sara..."

I hung up, grabbed my keys, and went to my mailbox. Maybe something there would take my mind off the previous night.

It finally happened. Yes, it's official, folks. The rite of passage had arrived. I just received the rudest piece of mail ever delivered to me:

Welcome to AARP. Our records show that you haven't yet registered for the benefits of AARP membership, even though you are fully eligible. As a member, you'll have the resources and information you need to get the most out of life over 50.

How did they find me? I've lied about my age for so long. They must have been tipped off by Social Security, another agency responsive to the needs of seniors. Was I in that club now? Once I joined the American Association of Retired Persons, it would be like putting one foot in the grave. Should I expect letters from the Neptune Society and Forest Lawn? Time's a wastin'…

3. Yoga Geezer
🐚🐚🐚

Julia took some time away from her Craigslist dates to go to yoga with me. At 52, she was blonde with sapphire blue eyes, fearlessly bisexual, and so comfortable being a sturdy, curvy 250 pounds, she often modeled in the Big Beautiful Woman catalogs.

We carried our mats up two flights of stairs to the sparse, hardwood-floored room. Rolling our mats out flat, not too close to the window, we placed our water bottles side by side. We each sat cross-legged, eyeing every young, beautiful woman who walked into the room, smiling at one another when we saw someone whose youthful beauty made us both feel ancient.

The teacher entered and the class began. Deep breathing, bending, flexing, and sweating, my mind concentrated on the movement of each limb in response to the commands of the teacher. Yoga is not about impressing anyone, gymnastic ability, or putting your foot behind your head. You are not required to be a woman, a Hollywood star, or a chanting vegetarian (though, if you live in L.A., you might find yourself wanting to be any of those for no apparent reason).

Today I focused within myself and didn't look at the gorgeous girls and former ballerinas half my age who could headstand with the ease of exhaling or touch their nose to their crotch effortlessly. I wiped the sweat from my brow, the back of my neck, and then glided into another asana. After an hour of pretzeled poses, it was time for "pigeon," which focuses on opening the hip flexors. This same part of the body is where holistic practitioners like Louise Hay believe we hold onto our deep-seated emotions and grudges.

It took me a while to position myself for pigeon, also known as humble warrior, as I aligned my body for optimum humble hip opening. I was agitated, clumsy, fumbling to get my feet and knees where they should be.

Finally, my pigeon was calm and aligned, or so I thought. The teacher approached and corrected my pose, gently pressing and pushing my sweaty limbs to stretch deeper, releasing into the asana.

The second after her adjustment, my mind clicked, as if a switch turned on a movie in my brain. It was a flashback to my married life, two decades ago. I saw myself younger, naked, straddling my then-husband Rupert in our bed. My head lifted up to the ceiling, and I screamed, like a mating call, releasing enough anger to shatter the ceiling as if it were a thin pane of glass.

Meanwhile, back on my yoga mat, I'm aware of a low groan — the same scream, only muffled, emitting from my mouth, echoing into my stomach. As I'm groaning, I feel my body release, as if years of angst were peeling away, melting, dissolving. I felt lighter and happier as I wiped a tear and switched to position the same pose on the other side of my body.

A half hour later, class ended. Julia and I smiled at one another, rolled up our mats, and walked to the back of the room to collect our shoes.

"You're quite the intense yogini," said Will, the only man in the class.

"Me?" I said, surprised to be noticed, let alone singled out.

"Yes, I heard you having a breakthrough on your mat," he nodded. "Most remarkable. I'm Will, by the way. I think I've seen you here before. But I'm usually surfing at this hour." Will was tall and lean, kind of a bean pole with a silvery mane of thick grey hair. His face was kind and lined, somewhere between 60 and 65, maybe older, but his body looked youthful, and his eyes were ageless.

"You surf?" I was surprised.

"Yes, I live a block from the beach. It's great to start the day with my board."

"I'm Sara. This is my friend Julia."

"Hello, ladies." Will fumbled with his mat to try and shake my hand. "Well, you two look like you're off somewhere together. I don't want to keep you…I was going to ask if you wanted to get some coffee."

Julia glanced at me, raised her eyebrows, cocked her head, and said, "We weren't going anywhere together. I'm going home to do my taxes. Why don't you two go for coffee?" She practically pushed me into him.

The next thing I knew, I was sitting at an outdoor café on a tree-lined street sipping a latte and hearing Will's life story. Was this moment like my first meeting with Ack, the only difference being the breed of dogs resting obediently at the foot of the next table? No, Will was a kinder, gentler human being. He was a doctor of infectious diseases, including AIDS, newly divorced with one daughter in college and the other living on her own, aged 30 — same age as some of my friends.

"I write self-help and some health-related articles, mainly about alternative healing and Eastern medicine. I've edited a book on AIDS," I offered, to show I was knowledgeable about the subject.

"I'm not that familiar with Eastern medicine. The trials are inconsistent."

"It helps people. Many treatments and modalities have helped bring AIDS patients into remission." I sipped my coffee, thinking I'd antagonized yet another first date, so I turned away from him, noticing the people with dogs strolling past our table.

"There's something very intriguing about you. I'd like to get to know you better." Will reached across the table to touch my hand. He was clearly handsome, a cross between Leonard Bernstein and Henry Fonda. But he had an old man's hand. It made me feel old, wondering if, as he touched me, I'd dry up, crack, and wither away.

Meanwhile, women of all ages, at other tables and passing by, looked at him admiringly. But I was still not sold on the idea of being with someone so much older. My first task was to surmise *how much* older he was. "Undergraduate school? How did you decide to become a doctor?" I was wearing my reporter/detective hat now.

"Undergraduate, Berkeley, where the best lefties are born and educated." He smiled, raising his cup to me. "I was always politically active. I wanted to march on Washington with Martin, but my parents said I was too young."

My mind raced to place "Martin," as in Luther King. Will wanted to march on Washington at a time when I was barely in elementary school and not allowed to cross the street myself! If I were better in history and math, I'd know his age. But I didn't want to ask because then I'd have to "give up" my real age, a secret that rivaled the mysteries of the pyramids.

I'm good at getting dates to talk about themselves. Will waxed poetic about the '60s, meeting his wife at a Black Panthers meeting (something all the really dedicated liberals did, along with a stint in the Peace Corps). He revealed himself to be a caring soul, passionate about his beliefs, living life true to himself, a goal most people just dreamed about. No, his wife was not a woman of color — she was a blonde, blue-eyed heiress and sometimes model — the trifecta of perfection.

His eloquent words about a long, interesting life were spoken through thin lips, with signs of age at the corners. His lined face was world-traveled. Every experience left its mark, and I saw them all facing me as we both sipped our coffee. He was the personification of what most women would call "a good catch" or "a keeper."

Still raw from the "Ack rejection", all I could see was a remarkable man, and fearing he'd find me unremarkable, I focused on his thin lips, old man hands, and my imagined newly divorced male need for sexual reawakening after a 32-year marriage (to a slim-thighed, golden goddess, or so I believed). Many of my friends have experienced the melodrama of being the first woman a man sleeps with after his long marriage ends. During that penis resurrection rite of passage, the woman is just a vessel for his need to act out and release the emotional angst of his divorce process. Rebound girl or teacher were not roles I wanted to play. I didn't want to be the woman whose job is to finalize a man's divorce and officiate his born-again, newly single stud life.

Since the sting of Ack the hack, I was leery of men eager to savor the juice of a sexy, younger woman. I was flattered by Will's attentiveness, yet felt neither sexy nor juicy. I am a prune on a date, in the disguise of a woman. I decided that this time it was me *not* jumping in with both feet, knowing full well I might be missing a great opportunity.

I smiled politely. "I should be going soon," I said tentatively, trying to think of the activity I should be going to so I could fashion a proper excuse.

"Me, too." He stood. "I'd like to see you again…maybe dinner?" Reaching into his pocket, Will pulled out two business cards. He asked for and wrote down my number on the one card, then gave me the other. "I'll be in touch." He reached for my hand and kissed it. We walked in opposite directions.

Will was classy, proper, handsome, well-mannered, and well-off. Why did he seem too old and wrong for me? In this case, I was the one who was shallow and rejecting, the very thing I'd accused Ack of being mere hours ago. I never wanted to think about the fact that I was old enough to have grown kids, or even be a grandmother. Will spent 32 years in a committed relationship, proof he knew how to do it. If I was really ready for a serious relationship, I'd focus on his years of service. Or would I?

Because I live in the veneer-soaked La La Land that is Los Angeles, I'd never dated a man whose kids were old enough to give him grandchildren. I'd always dated chubby Peter Pans and man-children, seldom a man *with* children and never one who saved lives. Plus, I realized Will was around Paul McCartney's age, close to retirement, collecting Social Security, and ready for a chapter in life far from where I was. I felt like I was out with someone's granddad, an attractive man who, even though I liked his company, I couldn't become attracted to, nor cuddle up to or be skin-to-skin with. Would I have felt that way with the real Paul McCartney?

I went home to rewrite my article, *Sex with your Ex, 10 Reasons to Say No* because my editor thought some of the true-life examples I'd collected from friends weren't believable enough. I needed to make up stuff to deliver and sell the piece. But since it was always difficult for me to rewrite, I began my work session the way I usually did, by focusing on everything else but writing. As soon as I got home, I watered the plants, did a load of laundry, paid some bills, fluffed and rearranged the pillows on the couch, and then called Julia.

"'I'm doing my taxes?!'" I blurted the second she said hello. "It's July. Why didn't you say you were shopping for a Christmas tree?"

"Well, how was coffee? If no one pushes you or hits you over the head, nothing happens," Julia fired back.

"He's okay." I said with indifference.

"He's handsome. Lots of charisma…like a maestro."

"Does he seem old to you?" I inquired.

"He's got vitality…vigor…that's good."

"He's a doctor."

"I knew he had vigor…and he can prescribe Viagra."

"He said he wants to see me again. I'd be fine if he didn't call. I'm not interested."

Julia said, "I think he holds great promise. I have a good feeling about this one."

"I know he seemed interested in me, but it felt creepy being touched by somebody older than Paul McCartney. I know you think he should be my 50th birthday gift to myself."

"Nothing's better than birthday sex!" she shot back.

"I don't like to screw on the first date."

"Sometimes that's not the best approach…but I am your sluttiest friend. Another suggestion, sign up for Facebook! That way everyone you've ever met in your entire life can find you, face you, and wish you a happy birthday."

"You mean that social website students and rock bands use?"

"I think you'll be pleasantly surprised. I bet you have old beaus, admirers, and others from your past eager to reconnect with you."

"More like lurking in the shadows."

"Lighten up. Try Facebook. If nothing else, you'll get birthday greetings from all over the country. Try it. Check out my page, then make one for yourself. I guarantee surprises. Do it today!"

I said goodbye to Julia just as another call was coming in — one of my other close friends, Lila.

"How is the almost birthday girl?" Lila asked cheerfully.

"I'm recuperating from last night's bad date, but somebody new picked me up at yoga today."

"In one door and out the other," she said. "I hope your dance card is free beginning in the morning, on your special day. "

"My birthday morning?"

"Yes, doll, I want to kidnap you and show you a good time."

"Sounds great," I said smiling.

"I'll pick you up at 8:30. And bring a bathing suit."

"Would I really have a good time in a bathing suit? My thighs have been declared a national disaster."

"I'm older, with more cellulite. Trust me. Be ready…I'll call when I'm five minutes away."

I hung up with Lila, turned on my computer, and went to Facebook.com. I'd thought about doing this for a while, but what better time than now? I could use a little diversion. I set up a profile and looked for Julia. Then I looked through her friends. Some of mine were there too. I contacted them. Then I searched for my best friend from high school and my high school boyfriend. Found both of them. Sent friend requests. They friended me immediately. I scrolled through their friends and saw people I knew so I contacted them. Fingers click-clacking on the keyboard, they sounded like the microwave popcorn I nuked, burned, and inhaled as dinner. My neck and shoulders ached from being hunched over in a secondhand desk chair. But by the time I went to sleep that night I had 35 friends!

4. Face the Music
♛♛♛

First thing in the morning Julia called me, blurting, the second I picked up the phone. "You must come to my house for pre-birthday cocktails, tonight at seven."

"That's very nice, but I...."

"You can't say no. No excuses. You have to be here," she insisted.

"Well, if I have no choice, what am I wearing?"

"Something comfortable. I know you have those 'eating pants' with the drawstring waist, and a cute top. See you at seven. Don't be late."

In anticipation of Julia-style fun and surprises, that afternoon I napped, showered, and set my hair on electric rollers, so I too could have the bouffant oomph of a soap opera actress like Julia usually did.

Arriving exactly at seven, I rang her doorbell. When she opened the door, a group of my friends, Beth, Lila, and Diana, were all sitting on couches. No one was drinking cocktails. No one said "Surprise."

Julia smiled and hugged me. Then, with a serious voice she said, "We're all here because we love you, care about your happiness, and want to help you."

This was more of a lead balloon than a birthday greeting. Something was stinky. There was a woman sitting in a club chair who I'd never met before. All eyes were on her. Molly, an unpretentious, soft spoken woman wearing beige separates, tasteful jewelry, and no make-up shook my hand.

"Sara, I've been brought here by your wonderful, loving friends," Molly began. "Everyone in this room wants to help you, and that's why they called me. Please sit down. I have a lot to share with you."

Looking around the room, there were my best girls all sitting close together, all silent, focused on this soothing-voiced stranger. I felt agitated, eager to bolt, yet somehow intrigued by this grouping of my friends exhibiting strange behavior.

"What is this, *Candid Camera*? Or are you putting me on a reality show? Which one of you thought that was a good birthday gift? Most of you don't even watch television. What's going on here?" I said, fear racing through me.

Julia put her arm around me and rubbed my shoulder, urging me to sit down next to her. The more she tried to soothe me, the less calm I felt. I looked down at the rug, not wanting to lock eyes with anyone, knowing they were all focused on me.

"Sara," Molly continued, softly but sternly. "I understand that you've had over 300 first dates without a relationship or loving experience. Your friends brought me here because they are concerned for you. They think you should have more jubilation in your life and less tribulations. "

"Am I dreaming this?" I blurted. "Is this what happens when a self-help writer doesn't take a vacation? She dreams her world is trying to fix her problems? Is Oprah in the bathroom waiting to fix my life, give me a cashmere sweater and a car? What the fuck is this, and who are you?"

"This is a relationship intervention. I'm a psychotherapist who specializes in sexual addiction…"

"This is a joke! Everyone here knows I'm the most celibate one in this room. This is the warm-up to the male stripper, right? You kids crack me up!"

"S-a-r-a," Molly said my name slowly and calmly, yet again. Now her soothing tone was irritating. "Your friends here tonight want you to be happy. They invited me to speak with you to help resolve some of your issues, so that you can lead a happier, healthier life. With your permission, we can explore the patterns that have caused you unhappiness and begin the healing. Do I have your permission?"

I looked around the room. All of my friends were nodding at me as if to say, "Say yes, say yes." No way, I thought to myself. How do I get out of this?

Diana, a tall, strong, voluptuous woman turning 60 soon, was the friend I've known the longest. She placed a large book on the coffee table. It was my wedding album. I shuddered from the shock of seeing that here, now.

Molly continued, "In dealing with patterns, we'll begin with your most significant relationship with men. We'll revisit your marriage."

The sound of her words sent nausea racing though me. I squirmed, eager to stand and leave. Julia held me down. She said, "Let's do this now, once and for all. Then you can be happy. Just listen to Molly."

Molly opened the wedding album, scanning each photo, then showing the pages to me. "You look more frightened than happy in these pictures. What were you thinking that day? Tell me about why you chose this man and how it ended."

I fidgeted in my seat, resistant, feeling straight-jacketed in the moment, burning to bolt out of there.

Julia whispered in my ear, "Just listen, and breathe. It will all be better soon."

I gulped, turning as Diana spoke, "Sara dated this guy for about a year. He was smart, funny, and good in the sack. He wanted to marry her. She didn't think anyone else would ever ask her. She thought the fun and good loving would continue. Neither did. As soon as they said I do, he didn't. They stopped doing anything together. He slept with five women in his office within the first year of marriage. He spent 100,000 dollars on horse racing. Sara felt she couldn't afford to stay."

"Ya know, this is as much fun as a colonoscopy. When's the birthday cake?"

"Your detachment shows how painful this issue still is for you. Unresolved angst is what's causing your current romantic challenges."

"I don't have a romantic life."

"We want you to," Lila chimed in. A blue-eyed blonde in her late 50s, she was wickedly wise and full of surprises. "We want you to have love and happiness and…"

"And lots of sex," Diana jumped in. "Listen to Molly. She's here to help you."

"The decisions about your next relationship were all colored by the unresolved issues from your marriage. You felt you couldn't trust your husband, and more importantly, you couldn't trust yourself. Think about it. Does this ring true?"

My friends looked at me like I was a puppy going in for surgery. It was embarrassing and painful to explore all of this now, in front of everyone. But my friends all knew me so well, so it felt more like one of those teaching surgeries, where all of the med students stand around observing and learning. I hoped the moment would do someone some good.

"It rings, like a car alarm that won't shut itself off," I blurted, distressed.

"What choices did you make in your next relationship?" Molly asked.

Beth stood to speak. At 45, Beth, the youngest of my friends, was married and had two sons, aged 17 and 20. She had short, dark hair and clear porcelain skin. She began, "That's a funky place in the way-back machine. Sara divorced at 29 and had a bunch of no-chemistry, not–even-a-kiss-on-the-first-date experiences till 32. Then she dated a guy whose mother had just died. He wanted Sara to redecorate her apartment with his mom's stuff. He'd bring her worn-out chairs with crooked arms and lots of doilies for her tabletops. She told me she never felt sexy, just old and dusty."

"Is this my birthday or my eulogy?" I said loudly and bitterly, boiling with frustration, feeling exposed and dissected like a bug under a microscope whose wings were being pulled apart.

I heard Julia giggle. My eyes darted to her immediately, like a nun spying a disobedient fifth grader.

"I'm sorry to laugh. But your hardships can be hilarious. I was just thinking about one."

"We're here so that Sara has happy relationships, not laughable hardships," Molly insisted, emphasizing the seriousness of the occasion. "What happened to the new relationship after your marriage?"

"Well, he did *want* to have sex with me, but only on his late mother's bed. Now if that wasn't creepy enough, over her bed was a life-size crucifixion, complete with blood on the cross. I so wanted to heal my feelings of being sexually abandoned by my husband with acts of sexual abandon. But this guy was sooooo not the choice. The minute he would get me to the bed, I would bolt from the room. After three times I realized I couldn't be touched by this man. So I ended the relationship."

"You walked out?" Molly asked, confirming my statement.

"I stumbled, in a running fashion, to be exact."

Now Lila was laughing. "Kid, I wish there was a male stripper here for you tonight. Sounds like you need it more than anybody."

Molly cleared her throat, as if trying to get the room back on track. "Why do you think you are single now?"

"Have you ever been on a dating website? Nightmare Alley. Water, water, everywhere and not a drop to drink. Most men want women under 40. That ain't me, babe. I missed the last bus out of single town about 10 years ago." I delivered that last line with a James Cagney accent.

"I'm familiar with web dating research. Yes, 51 percent of men want women of childbearing age. But 49 percent of older men are eager for relationships with older women."

"Not in Los Angeles. Every balding, potbellied divorced guy with a late-model car feels entitled to date an actress or supermodel," I fired back.

"Did you ever think they can sense your anger and frustration, and that's why they recoil? That's the way the rest of the animal kingdom would react. Do you think you appear reserved or uptight?" Molly inquired.

"I don't think so. But I'm not on the receiving end of meeting me."

"Maybe you should explore what meeting you is like," Molly said. Her kind, even tone disguised accusations of my behavior with unwavering kindness. It made me want to punch her in the face. That's why it's called painful truth. "We know you want your dates to like you and meet your needs. But what do you bring to them? What do you offer of yourself?"

"I'm cute and funny. I have nice hair, especially tonight."

"Do you want dates to like the wrapping or the whole package?" Molly asked.

"All of me." I answered, finally getting serious.

"Good answer," Molly smiled.

"You mean I got one right? I hope there will be some drinking tonight. This chat is ripping my guts out. Not the way I wanted to turn 50."

"How did you want to spend it?"

"In the loving arms of my life partner."

Diana jumped in, assertive but tender, "You look for love with such hunger — like there's a famine — and you'll shrivel up and die if you don't find someone."

Julia added, "I know I spend too much time on websites myself. I'm there for immediate gratification, an afternoon of lust and oven cleaning, not a lifetime supply of heart-pounding love. I have much lower expectations. That's what I'd recommend."

Lila spoke next, "We always cheer you on. We see you get all charged up — then stumble through hopes and expectations being dashed, horror stories, rejection, defeat, retreat. You fall and get up again, like a baby first learning to walk. We don't want to see you fall down again. It's not cute like a baby falling; it's just sad. Every time things end and you fall, I just want to hold and rock you till the hurt goes away."

Beth continued, "The shoemaker's wife has no shoes. The self-help writer gets help today — to find herself — and feel the love she already has in her life."

Julia, changing the mood said, "We were gonna do this or get you a male escort. But we couldn't agree on your type. Fred Flintstone was not available."

"That ex-husband created such a black mark on your life," Diana said. "Crooked-dicked twerp."

"How does she know he has a crooked dick?" Julia asked.

"I described it in detail in a moment of rage," I fired back.

"Diana gets the good dirt and I get the fat-girl college stories. We just don't want to see you suffer," Lila added.

Molly, eager to regain everyone's focus, said, "Sara, what if you cranked back your expectations and instead of looking for a life partner, if you were open to, say, a weekend companion, or someone you could be happy spending time with, sharing laughter with, building intimacy, rather than thinking like an architect and drawing up the plans for the rest of your life?"

"I'm listening," I said. My friends were smiling at me, eager to see resolution and for me to feel at ease.

Molly added, "We're here to help you rethink your choices and goals. Moving forward, think about being happy, day by day — not in pursuit of a band of gold. You know what I mean."

Everyone looked at Diana and giggled. Molly looked at her too, eager for an explanation.

"Molly, they're laughing 'cause I've had four husbands. I'm hoping for a fifth to get me though my old age," Diana remarked.

Molly turned back to me. "I hope you'll see this as helpful for you. Don't look for love in a be-all, end-all way. Look for good times and happiness today. A good evening, a good weekend, a responsive lover, these are the elements of a happy, healthy life."

"Just get laid," Diana snapped.

"Get happy," Lila added.

"Get laid. That will make you happier," Julia theorized. "You can write about it for magazines and make money. More sex, more money."

"Don't limit sex just to men either. You know I believe variety keeps life interesting," Beth chimed in with a wink. "I have some birthday plans in mind for you."

"If you can go out in the world with an eye towards just having a good time, I think you'll love life more," Molly said, smiling.

"When you're not trying so hard, it's easier to get laid," said Diana. "That's how it always works for me. You know I find a hot man whenever I need one."

"If you can agree to relax about your goals and expectations, we're here to help you have more happiness in your life and heat in your bed," said Julia. "I'll be like an AA sponsor. You can call me whenever you need something. We can go more places and meet new people, all kinds of people."

"So you all think that by trying too hard I've avoided relationships?"

Unanimous from the room: "Yes!"

"Really? Well, then maybe I *should* give up on searching for a relationship and just have a good time."

"Finally she gets it," Diana says, standing. "Now can we get that blender going with margaritas? We've all worked hard tonight."

"Girls just wanna have fun. Fun leads to sexual escapades. That keeps you young, happy, and chock-full of article ideas you can sell," Beth chimed in enthusiastically.

"Does anyone have a roadmap to fun?" I remarked cynically, thirsty, and ready for my chilled margarita.

5. Soakin' It Up

The following morning, my birthday, I woke up and felt old before I opened my eyes. My throat was dry and sore. Itchy eyes. I glanced at the clock, numbers blurry. I reached for a leg to see if it needed shaving. My skin felt parched, too. It was official. My first morning as a 50-year-old and I was drying up!

As I prepared my coffee, I thought about how in caveman days, nobody survived to be 50. So waking up, I was already ahead of the game. I'd finally recovered from a fat adolescence, but felt pudgy and more klutzy than sexy. People said 50 was the new 30. Thirty was good. I had great friends, a promising future, and bags of hope. Twenty years later, I was single with great friends, a sketchy future, and saddlebags. As I packed for the day, I thought, "Birthday. Bathing suit. Who thought putting those together was a good thing?"

I signed on to my computer just to check email. No working today! On Facebook, 20 of my "friends" had sent me birthday wishes. I'd received seven new friend requests while I was sleeping. The thought of being this popular without leaving the house made me feel warm and hopeful, with a little bit of strangeness at the same time.

One of the new requests was from Derrick, a guy I took classes with in college, but who I hardly knew. We never did more than have tea on a rainy day. I friended him and sent a note stating, "Nice to hear from you."

Lila arrived, smiling, arms outstretched for a warm hug. "Buckle up for adventure, birthday girl. Life begins at 50." As I got into the passenger seat, she belted an enthusiastic, off-key chorus of *"Happy Birthday."* My inner 11-year-old filled with glee. "If you didn't bring sunscreen, I have SPF 15, 25, and 65 — liquid burka."

Driving, we listened to the *Eagles' Greatest Hits. Take it easy… don't let the sound of your own wheels drive you crazy…* Good advice. I hoped I could listen.

After 90 minutes of Lila driving her minivan like a Ferrari, we arrived at Glen Ivy Hot Springs in Temecula. Lila parked in the first spot near the entrance. She had a handicapped sticker, or as she called it, "a gimp tag." At 56, she'd already had two near-death experiences, including a car accident that left her with a limp and need of a cane — but looking at her face, one would never guess. Her winning smile framed champagne blonde hair and sparking blue eyes that shined sexy and experienced. Lila's carefree laugh belied her painful past. Her courage and perseverance were a life lesson to me. The wisest and worldliest of my friends, we had worked together at my first corporate job, where she helped me navigate the shark-infested waters. I'd always clamored for her wisdom, doled out preciously like pearls.

I was excited to be entering the unpretentious spa, also known as Club Mud. We walked to the dressing room and readied ourselves for our day of relaxation. In the bathroom, I squirmed and tugged into a one-piece black suit, took a quick glance in the mirror, and (as always) tried not to hate my thighs. I've had an issue with my thighs since my fat adolescence. I still struggled with overeating. If I could just lose those last damn 10 pounds, I'd be queen of my universe — and my life would be perfect. Yeah, right. And the minute I lose those 10 pounds, George Clooney will come to my house, give me a stripper-gram, and carry me off to his house in Lake Como, Italy.

While dressing, my eyes darted around the dressing room, taking inventory of other women disrobing — exposing their breasts, hips, bellies. All different shapes and sizes, each with her own unique beauty. I found something attractive and admirable about every woman I saw. And I started to feel aroused by my thoughts. The last time I had these feelings I was in the group bathroom of my college dorm. But I'd never acted on it, including the night one of my floor mates drank too much and gave me a long, lingering hug that crossed the line of blossoming into a kiss.

In college I felt intrigued, but afraid of being judged and rejected regarding all sexual experiences — this was true for my attractions to men and was doubly true of my desires for women. I wanted to share affection with women I admired — friends, the outspoken classmates in the women's studies program, even teachers. I was fascinated by intelligent women, magnetized by their inner power.

But fear of what people would think, or what my family might say, stopped me from acting on those feelings — then.

But now — I was at an age where no one was looking or thinking about what I was doing. Most of my judgmental family was dead. Many women my age dive into life eager for pursuits they've put on hold or thought about for years: marathon running, cooking school, or living on a desert island. On my way out to the sunshine I thought, "Fifty is the rebirth to go after what you've always wanted! I should write an article about it — or maybe begin by living bigger, louder, and bolder in pursuit of greater passion." I said to Lila, "Fifty and fearless. Time for new beginnings."

Towels, sun hats, sunscreen, and trashy magazines in tow, we marched to claim two lounge chairs. We positioned our possessions to indicate that these chaises were taken because it was the perfect spot — not too sunny, not too shady. I began to see my life as a giant swimming pool where I should be eager to jump in, splash around, and experience pleasure, as we strolled to the 'champagne mineral pools.'

Dunking in the pool, soaking up the warmth of the water, Lila said, "I'm surprised at myself for being here today. Nobody could get me into a bathing suit but you, Sara. This water feels good on my saggy skin and old bones."

"We have to promise ourselves…no smack talk about age today. Otherwise we might as well drown ourselves," I added, laughing.

A young woman with an accent was searching the mineral pools, asking for…ME! "Sara Rosen? It's time for your massage."

"Me? I didn't book a massage."

"I booked it for you," said Lila.

Arriving at the massage building, a small prefab bungalow, the young woman led me down a long hall, introduced me to a tall man, then bowed and excused herself.

"Ms. Rosen, please follow me," said this six-foot three-inch blue-eyed Swedish warrior god named Erich. He led me to my own private sanctuary. "I'll knock in three minutes," he said as he left me to undress.

I was thrilled, anticipating lying on a table, being touched and stroked all over, every inch of me oiled, caressed, and attended to. Everything was crisp, pristine, and white. I stripped off my bathing suit, hung it on a hook behind the door, and dove in naked between the cool sheets.

Right on time, Erich knocked and entered the room. He clicked on a CD boom box with some Yanni-type New Age music. He reached for a bottle of massage oil, squeezed some out, and warmed it with his hands before he even touched me. Erich stroked away tensions, knots, and tightness for almost an hour, seldom speaking.

Shortly after closing my eyes, at first, my mind raced: thoughts of work. There were never enough freelance writing assignments to feed a more than financially struggling life. Finally, as his hands rhythmically stroked my limbs, I relaxed into a trance-like state, recollecting a lover's desire, the heat and passion of a romantic encounter. My senses felt as parched as my skin.

When the massage was almost complete, Erich said, "I understand today is your birthday. Your friend has provided for a more extensive massage than our usual standard Swedish procedure. She wants you to have the most thorough full-body massage possible. Do I have your permission?"

"Sure," I shrugged, anticipating more deep tissue massaging on my shoulders and neck. Instead, Erich's hand caressed my thigh...my upper thigh. His skillful fingers made their way between my legs, probing, exploring, and then...

"His fingers are inside me!" I said to myself in disbelief, surprised, concerned, aroused. My limbs tightened. Was this legal? Should this be happening? Should I let it happen? It felt pretty good. Oooh, very good. I melted, opening.

"Be in the moment and enjoy it," I reprimanded my brain. That was always a challenge for me, thinking too much about the next moment, or the one five minutes in the future or past, while glossing over the present. It had been years since a man had touched me there. "Shut up and relax."

Pleasure surged, my arms and legs tingled. Heart pounding, I felt young and fresh-from-the-box new, not thinking or complaining or reflecting or feeling dried up.

Breathing deeply, tuning into the moment, senses energized as his fingers moved deeply, gentle at first, then fast, faster, slower, then faster again until the ping-ting of the music was drowned out by my own outcries of pleasure and release. Ecstatic, this was exactly what I had needed. I felt like I'd robbed a bank and escaped with the loot.

When I floated out of the massage suite, dazed and delighted, I saw Lila sitting at a big round table with a beach umbrella, festive plates of food in front of her.

"How was your massage? Hope it had a happy ending," she remarked, laughing. "I thought the best gift for your birthday was to be rubbed the right way. Let's hope you don't have to wait until next year for it to happen again."

"Isn't this illegal?" I asked, thrilled to be pleasured anonymously. Though I'd never think of procuring a "happy ending" myself, I was delighted she had orchestrated my full-body birthday pleasure event.

"Anybody can be bought for cash under the table," Lila explained. "I do it all the time for my clients."

"You really are thoughtful." I hugged her. "Thank you. That was more memorable than a Target gift card."

"Found your target, didn't we?" Lila said, chuckling.

"Bull's eye," I blushed. "It was great. At first I didn't know what to think."

"The key to sexual pleasure is not thinking," she said. "And knowing what you want. What is it for you, Sara?"

I was silent. What were my sexual wants? I always saw sex in the context of a relationship — and since that had been elusive, sex had been on the back burner for so long, I forgot how to "cook." My face saddened searching for a memory to reflect on.

"Don't think about it too much. I ordered you a chicken Caesar and a cranberry juice," Lila said. After lunch, we headed to our lounge chairs for more trashy reading, a glorious nap, and then back in the mineral pool. "Are you having a good time?"

"That was really memorable. And nobody had to buy anyone dinner," I said smiling, still tingling and re-running the event through my mind.

"Sex with a partner was so last century for me," Lila tossed off, a sense of nostalgia to her aside. "You should be open to new experiences," she suggested gently. "I think the older we get, the less available men there are, the more it makes sense to consider the company of women. Even Margaret Mead said that as women live longer, it's an anthropological evolution to be with another woman. And she had a few husbands. The friendship of women grows deeper as we mature. If it turns sexual, there's more tenderness and compassion than fumbling around with some old man attached to a limp dick."

"Enough. You refuse to ever mention your husband. What is he, a hit man? How is he?" I asked.

"Far away, in Florida, the man boob and draggy ass capital of America. He's out of sight and out of mind, only calls when he needs something. He's not going anywhere — that's my problem. I'm too lazy to get a divorce. I see my horse's ass of a husband for holidays. We're buddies now, that's all. So, I have an excuse not to date, a poor excuse, one I send a monthly check to." We chuckled.

"Well, there's the company of women, which we both like," I explained. "And there's keeping company with women, touching another woman's body?"

Lila said, "It's been so long since I've been touched. I barely remember what it feels like to be kissed, to know the softness of someone's mouth on mine, or even their lips on a shoulder, let alone anywhere down south."

In this moment, I wanted to hold Lila, caress and console her, be the warm body to comfort her. I was certain any gesture like that from me would be fiercely rejected. Being a caring friend and being a lover was a boundary that seemed uncross able. Whenever I was with Lila, I wondered momentarily about that leap because I thought there was a scent of sexual tension between us.

"We've both been married. We <u>are</u> straight," I said, tentatively. "The men I meet tell me we have no chemistry. What they mean is that I don't make their dicks hard. At their age, no one makes their dicks hard, but they blame us. Without a little blue pill, most mid-life men are limp noodles. The main reason men get married is because they can only hold their farts in for so long," I laughed. "Men who are hot to marry women our age are ready for adult diapers. During foreplay, instead of moaning 'Oh baby,' I'll moan, 'Grampa, still breathing?'" Feeling sad, I added, "Yet, I want to find someone…"

"After last night's group hug about your love life, I thought you wanted to take things easier. New birthday, new beginnings. The very things we were afraid of and running from all these years might offer great comfort and joy when we least expect it."

"I'd like to lose some of my cynicism — or at least believe it's not too late to be happy. I have one last bit of hope left," I added, walking back to dunk in another pool.

"That's a good wish. That's my wish for myself. May I share it with you?" Lila asked, while adjusting the straps of her suit. We each found a spot in the mineral pool.

"Sure. I want to believe that at our age, if we fall in love, we won't break a hip," I joked. Was my wish realistic or a dream? Last night I agreed to just let life surprise me — could I do it?

"Today is about celebration — birthday, joy, and beauty. So lighten up!" she said.

"At 16, I could enter a room and everyone looked at me," I remembered aloud.

Lila splashed me with warm water and said, "Honey, if you want to go into the way-back machine, I was at Woodstock, shirtless, boobs bouncing in the breeze, listening to Janis Joplin. I was from the peace and love crowd, the free love generation! Now I can't give it away."

"I stopped dating bald men," I said triumphantly. "I liked going to the movies with them because if I needed to pee in the middle of the film, I'd always find my way back. I just used their head as a row marker."

"Age has a cruel sense of humor," Lila said. "My boobs are racing so fast to my knees, my bra needs a speedometer."

6. Out-Night Girls
☙ ☙ ☙

With less than a half century left, I wanted to cram a lot of living and loving in before I was in desperate need of a walker and/or my only companion was a home health aide.

Still recuperating from the Ack debacle and the close encounter with Molly the relationship counselor, I was having a restless, lazy Saturday, so I called Beth. She always had boundless energy — enough to lead a double life as a married bisexual, making it look effortless and highly desirable. I'd have to get one fully baked life before I could even consider a second.

Beth was free for dinner, so I threw on sneakers and a jacket and ran out the door to meet her at the Burbank mall. As soon as I parked near our designated spot by the muffler repair shop, I saw her dirty forest green minivan, fingerprinted windows and all. She honked and I ran for the passenger door.

Before I could buckle my seat belt, I blurted, "I have so much to tell you."

Beth kissed my cheek and giggled, "Careful, we're not alone."

I looked in the back of the van — and there sat Adam, Beth's teenaged son; his girlfriend Jane; Ricky, the drummer of their band; Fred, the guitarist; and all of their instruments. My eyes widened with surprise as everyone laughed.

"You forget I'm a mom," Beth said, laughing, driving, drinking soda, and brushing the bangs out of her eyes. "I'm taking the band to their sound check for tonight's show. I thought we'd hang for a while, listen to a few songs, and then go off on our own." She winked slyly.

"You're the mom. The mom with the most-est," I said.

"She's a cool rock 'n' roll mom," Jane exclaimed. The band nodded in agreement.

Beth and I helped the kids unload their instruments. We all marched into the dimly lit bar; the kids made a beeline for the stage. I watched the boys unwrap cords and connect guitars to amplifiers. As we watched the band set up, I reminisced, "Beth, I remember reading stories to Adam and we sang songs while he beat a pot with a wooden spoon."

"Now he has a girlfriend who sleeps over," Beth replied as she got us each a beer. "I'm a mom to teenagers. Sometimes I can't believe my life."

"I know. Sometimes I can't believe your life either."

We listened to the band rehearse two songs, finished our beers, said our goodbyes, and were back in the minivan.

"Now I'll take you to the kind of bar I like," said Beth, switching on the ignition. As the sun set, we arrived at a small, boxy building that could have been anything. The parking lot was half full. Beth smiled as she locked the car and put her arm around me. We walked to the club, and Beth held the door open for me. "Welcome to my world!"

It looked like any bar I'd been to — loud music, people talking, laughing, and drinking. Only here, everywhere I looked, I saw women — just women, every age, shape, and size. Sure, a few had short hair and looked kind of unfeminine, but many were breathtakingly beautiful with long hair and centerfold-worthy bodies.

"Here, I got you a beer. Let me show you around." Beth winked, taking my arm. I was a tourist in her side-life, and she was guiding me through her favorite sights. I could tell she relished the surprise on my face — and I must have looked like a visitor to a foreign country, marveling at the attractions. As much as I heard Beth talk about this part of her life, I'd never been to the places she hung out or met the women she knew, until now. "Here's the dance floor. There are the pool tables," she pointed, sipping, smiling. "I love it here, my home away…from the boys."

I'd never seen Beth so happy. Her eyes darted to every woman within her view. "Beth, this is definitely… something," I said. We clinked bottles.

"You can't find the words, but you will," she laughed. "I see someone I know. Come with me and say hello."

I took a hard swallow of my beer and followed Beth. She hugged a woman named Theresa, an accountant at a construction company. I shook her hand. Theresa had a strong handshake — and a winning smile. The two began an animated conversation. I felt like a third wheel in a private moment, so I excused myself to the ladies room. In there, two women were kissing while another woman reapplied her lipstick and combed her hair. "There's every kind of woman here," I thought to myself. "Maybe I'll see someone for me."

The club was more crowded now, so it was difficult to get the bartender's attention. I leaned in between two women sitting at the bar, but I was still ignored.

"What are you drinking?" asked the woman on the stool to my right. She was dressed all in black, had waist-length blonde hair, resembling Joni Mitchell in her *Ladies of the Canyon* days.

"Amstel Light."

"Debra, two Amstel Lights," she said, getting the bartender's attention immediately. Before I could say anything, Debra swiftly delivered the two beers. I reached for my pocket. "No, honey. This one's on me," she told me, with a mere nod of her head to Debra indicating to put it on her tab.

"Wow, thank you," I said, studying the woman's pretty face. "I'm Sara." "I'm Corinne." She clinked my bottle with hers. "I live three blocks away," Corinne said, now studying my face. "And you?"

"I'm here with my friend Beth." I broke her gaze to look around the room. I saw Beth dancing with Theresa. "Beth's over there," I said, pointing to the dance floor.

"Wanna dance?" Corinne asked, standing and taking my hand. I tried to act as if this was something I always did. I took two hard swallows of beer and followed Corinne to the dance floor. Beth caught my eye and nodded approvingly. The music was easy dancing disco tunes, Michael Jackson from Off the Wall, then Donna Summer's Last Dance. I moved to the music, holding my beer — and Corinne's gaze. I gulped more beer between each song — not because I was thirsty; I needed to ease the heat in the room. I was a nervous stranger in a strange land. I stared at the bartender, wondering if she could tell I was a "newbie", some woman otherwise out of her element. Would I be found out and asked to leave?

Marvin Gaye's <u>Sexual Healing</u> — a slow song — began to play. Corinne took the bottle from my hand and placed it on a counter. With her other hand, she encircled my waist, gently placing her hand on my back. After about a minute of dancing, she slowly drew me closer. I fidgeted a bit, trying to keep rhythm with the music, anxious that a beautiful woman wanted to hold me tight and flirt with me. Corinne nuzzled my neck. I felt her heated breath near my ear and smelled her freshly shampooed hair. My heart pounded with excitement and uncertainty. My head and neck broke out in a sweat. The music now sounded like garbled voices underwater. Was I afraid or aroused? Or both? I didn't remember this song having such a drum beat — oh wait — that was my heart pounding. Could she feel it? Attraction or fear? Or fear of attraction?

When the song ended, I asked to go back to the bar for some ice water. Corinne got it for me in seconds, and two more beers as well. We talked and drank, sitting on side-by-side bar stools. This all seemed surreal, worlds away from any moment in my real life. It was a play, a theater piece in a dark bar, and I was a character, a nervous virgin far from home.

Corinne stroked my hair. My arms twitched like a marionette whose strings were pulled too quickly. Stroking her hair, I took a long breath and then complimented her long golden mane. The moment felt terrifyingly tense, weirdly unfamiliar, yet happy. It was warmer and more caring than recent dating experiences; I was eager and open to see where this would lead. I decided, if I copied everything she did, like a mirroring exercise in acting class, I'd be fine. She wouldn't know I'd never done this before.

I saw Beth at the other side of the bar with Theresa and another woman. Our eyes met. She toasted me with her bottle. Corinne ordered two more beers, still refusing to let me pay. By now, I'd had more beers than usual and had lost count. The room was getting hotter and more crowded as it filled to capacity, brimming with women. I wiped the sweat from my brow, embarrassed to be visibly heating up. I held the chilled beer bottle to my temple for some relief.

"I don't want you passing out. Let's go to the back garden," said Corinne. She tilted her head, using the same gesture she used to get the bartender's attention. Fresh air in the breezy black night cooled me down immediately. There were women whispering, smoking, and getting cozy together. I cooled myself off more with the beer, first holding the bottle to my neck, then drinking it down like water.

She took her bottle and held it to the back of my neck, leaned in, and grazed my cheek with her lips. As electricity raced down my spine, the rest of me felt numb. In this moment, realizing I was drunk, she kissed my mouth. I kissed her in return. Corinne's passionate lips were now exploring my mouth and tongue as her breasts pressed up against mine. It was a first kiss that seemed intuitive and more thoughtful than a man's lips would feel.

Suddenly, something was in my throat, as if I was being choked from the inside. I pulled away and gasped for air. Thinking it was fear, I swallowed hard, then tried to cough away the tightness. Instead, I threw up all the beers Corinne had bought me. I was mortified; she was horrified.

"I'll get someone to clean this up." Corinne flew back into the club. I stood still as a statue until someone arrived with a mop and bucket. Then I slowly walked back inside. Corinne was gone. Beth was looking for me.

I drank ice water, and then Beth drove us back to our real lives. In the car I was silent, simmering in my humiliation.

"Did you have a good time?" quizzed Beth in a motherly tone. I remained silent, replaying the night's events through my mind, wincing. Beth added, "You were drinking and dancing and kissing…that's a good time."

"And after that stare-fest of an intervention my good friends ambushed me with, that's what I'm supposed to be doing, right? I guess that group grilling paid off. So maybe I did have a good time, until I behaved like a buffoon. They'll hang my photo in the restroom, captioned "Heterosexual puker, stay away!"

"It's just beginner's bad luck," Beth offered.

"I kissed a girl and I threw up!" I replied despairingly.

"It happens to the best of us," Beth replied kindly.

"No, it doesn't. Hetero puker, a new disaster film with girl-on-girl action where an ingénue blows chunks. What an Oscar-worthy crowd pleaser. My dating pool is getting so small; soon it will be a shot glass!"

7. Back In the Game
※ ※ ※

The morning after "Dyke Bar Disaster" I checked my email. I received six Facebook notifications, including one from Derrick. I signed onto Facebook to see what he had to say. He'd sent me photos of his two pre-teen daughters and the tree house he built for them. I wrote to him: 'Pretty daughters, nice tree house. Sweet, idyllic life. Wife?'

Checked my regular email. Found one from Diana that read:

Hey, Sara, guess what happened over the weekend? I was fed up with life and so was my friend Karla, so we went to Brophy's on the pier in Santa Barbara. I met an Israeli man. He was bald, heavy, short, interesting, and very, very rich. He asked me out that night. He's called me twice since then. Maybe I'm back in the game...

I called Diana. "Male attention again? You, with a short Israeli?"

She laughed. "When he stands on his money, we're both the same height."

"Do you like him?" I asked. "Was he a good date?"

"He's a bull in a china shop — gruff, uncultured, demanding. He took me to dinner and God knows what's next."

"What do you *want* next?" I asked. "You've had more men lusting after you than any woman I know. Attention from men is the greatest high for you."

"He didn't push me to sleep with him," replied Diana, confident of her red-hot sexual energy. "He got a peck on the cheek and that was it — not that he didn't want to come home with me. I don't know what this is all about, but I'm getting fat."

"I guess you won't want to do lunch with me tomorrow then?" I asked.

Diana said, "I'll meet you. Let's go to that Mexican place in Agoura Hills."

Next day Diana arrived stylishly late. Dressed to flaunt her figure, she wore white cotton pants that hung on her tushless, boyish behind and billowed around her ice skater's legs. On top, she wore a slinky, black V-neck sweater, revealing her ample cleavage with proud assurance. Flaxen hair framed her welcoming face, giant eyes, and animated smile. The thing I liked most about her Diana-ism: we spent so much time talking about her life and problems that my own concerns seemed miniscule.

Before we ordered, Diana said, "The Israeli called last night. It was a long night of sex, wine, and worship. I didn't think he had it in him, but he sure had it in me!"

"You enjoy men, all men, don't you?" I asked purposefully.

"They light me up and make me feel alive…vibrant. The younger they are, the more alive I feel," she said.

"I'm so tired of hearing men say that about women," I replied.

"There's something about the electricity of a passionate man, Sara…"

"I feel so caught up in your dates. I get a vicarious thrill — you're going through it all, so I don't have to."

Don't you miss the pleasure, lust, and the laughter?" Diana asked. "A man's skin and his heat on you? What about the adventure of a new man and all of his surprises?"

Chips and margaritas arrived at the table. I crunched hard at the thought of male heat and its surprises. I tried hard to picture myself in a happy, intimate moment with a man. No image came to mind. Instead, my body tensed, my blood raced, and I squirmed in my chair. I painfully remembered my night with Ack and felt nauseous.

"Recently, I find men's surprises to be disappointments," I said, wiping salsa from the corner of my mouth.

"You used to date up a storm, always someone new."

"Beau du jour," I responded, smiling weakly.

"That's the Sara I know. Who have you been up to lately?"

"I went out to a bar with Beth," I said.

"A dyke bar? I don't know how she does it. Or why you'd want to do it. I've known you since you were 25. You're not a lesbian," said Diana, sipping her drink. "You're just going through a dry spell with men. Don't stress. It'll change. I know there's a husband in your future — and mine, too. No friend of mine could be a lesbian. Just stick with dick and you'll be fine."

Driving home, I thought about men's bodies, the physical presence of men in my life — and in my bed. I thought about men caressing my body. That kind of sexual experience seemed worlds away. The mere thought of it was as if I were watching a foreign film of my sex life, but on the screen, I saw me sitting on a couch, looking pretty, waiting…just waiting. I heard sounds of people talking and laughing in the next room, as if a party was taking place. No one walked past me or even entered my room. I wasn't sure where I should look.

Cut to another film — Corinne kissing me. I don't feel drunk or nervous, just good. Then the film breaks, the projector has overheated. The film is melting — screen goes to black. Even my imagination doesn't give me a break — or a thrill.

Back in the real world, I had an article due. I was too busy helping women 18 to 35 solve their problems to think about my own dilemmas. I went home to begin the piece: *Are You Ready for a New Relationship?* I couldn't find my notes anywhere. Instead, I located bank statements from 1986, photos from a friend's wedding (we lost touch after their first child was born, no surprise) and some letters I'd received from my dad's friends shortly after he died. I sat and read them and cried. One thing I knew for sure: If I wasn't ready to write an article about having a new relationship, I surely wasn't ready to have one. So instead I outlined the other piece I was on deadline for: *19 Mistakes Women Make When They're Dating A New Man.* This was as easy as chewing gum.

What Women Do Wrong That Causes Promising Relationships to Die Out

They jump into relationships too fast.

They want commitment too fast.

They overdress.

They wear too much make-up.

They talk too much.

They talk too little.

When writing went badly, I felt restless. When it went well I felt anxious. Either way, the results were the same. I developed a burning desire to focus on anything but writing. I did a load of laundry. I went to my mailbox and found two bills and some takeout menus. There was another envelope. On one side it had a color photo of a beautiful woman reclining at a beach. The line of copy asked, *"How comfortable should 50 be?"* I was mortified. Did the entire world know my age and insist on taunting me, assaulting my vanity? I opened the envelope and read:

50. Feels good, doesn't it? But what do you want for the future? 50 more healthy years? Financial security? An AARP membership can help.

Shortly after AARP found me, solicited, and sucker-punched my psyche asking for membership, I was still reeling from being qualified to join a support group for the senior population. They moved pretty quickly and aggressively for a bunch of oldsters.

I went back upstairs, checked my email, and learned that three of my new story ideas had been rejected. And I'd be receiving a kill fee (only a third of my usual rate) for a relationship story where the publisher decided they wanted a man's point of view — and a man to write it. Ah, the bleak world of rejection and the freelance writer. To take my mind off of my disappointments, I called Diana, hoping more of her Diana-isms could distract me from my inertia and rejection.

"I may have found a husband…for YOU!" she blurted.

"For me?" I gulped down a glass of water as my emotions raced from hope to horror. "Was that on my Christmas list? I thought I'm just supposed to have a good time. No relationship goals, no husband hunting."

Diana continued, "One of my friends from my last job has a brother, Roberto. He's an opera singer, a tenor, cultured, with a few extra pounds — your type. He travels a lot, but a week from Sunday, you're meeting him at her house, for brunch."

"Brunch next week with someone I haven't even spoken to?" I was anxious for a multitude of reasons.

"Trust me, I know what you like," Diana said, with certainty. "I said glowing things about you. My goal is to get you married."

8. My Late Date
🐚🐚🐚

For Sunday brunch I dressed in soft colors and applied pretty pink lip gloss. I wanted to look as youthful and girlish as possible. Suzy Condella's home was a large English Tudor estate in Encino; rolling lawns, lots of trees, and no sidewalks. I walked to the front door eager and hopeful despite myself, straightening my clothes and hair before ringing the bell. Suzy came to the door wearing jeans and a black t-shirt. Although she was smiling, her eyes looked sad and red, as if she'd been crying.

"Sara? We've been expecting you. Please come in." Suzy shook my hand and ushered me down a short hallway into a gigantic, spotless kitchen. "Please sit. I have something to tell you." What could a total stranger have to tell me? I swallowed hard, maintaining her gaze. "You won't be meeting my brother today," she began. "He was driving home from San Diego and…" Her voice broke. "He had a fatal heart attack. Only 55 years young. My brother is gone. The funeral was two days ago."

I stood, thinking: Funeral? My date died before I even met him! I thought it best to excuse myself. This felt like being somewhere between a fever dream and a David Lynch film

— soon my feet would feel heavy, a midget would enter, and someone would get amnesia. I tried to focus on the moment while wondering if anyone who cooked could actually keep this kitchen so spotless.

"Oh, don't go. You were invited for brunch. Diana has told me so much about you. Please join the rest of the family. They're poolside, waiting for you."

I winced at the thought of dining with my dead date's family…but she insisted — and feeling trapped by the circumstances, my heart going out to those in such pain, I followed Suzy out the back door and greeted <u>seven</u> other relatives of the late Roberto.

Sitting under an umbrella, drinking an umbrella drink, conversing with the family of my late date, I marveled at the absurdity of it all. Why was I here? This table full of strangers working through their grief was nevertheless warm and cordial. How I wished I'd met them under other circumstances. I longed for a family like this. There were advantages to being a dead guy's girlfriend. He seldom embarrassed you in front of friends. You always knew where he was. If only we'd met while he was…breathing.

Despite a lovely lunch, I didn't linger. I thanked everyone profusely, with hugs and kisses on both cheeks. Driving home, my mind raced faster than the other drivers on the 101 freeway, thinking about an article I wrote years ago about the worst blind date I'd ever had — he committed suicide three hours before the date. Another late date? Was that a story-worthy article title? I'd write it up when I got home. But what really happened today? Did it count as a date, or anything resembling a date? Was this a sign I wasn't *really, really* ready for a new relationship? Or was it just another odd life experience I'd turn into a freelance paycheck? After my AARP harassing, gentle reminder, I realized I had less than half a century left. NOW was the lightning round of MY game show. The best future possible was the champion's prize. I was afraid I'd only win the washer/dryer, or even worse, a year's supply of Rice-a-Roni.

I drove lost in feelings of aloneness, aware of my own transience, eager to make every moment matter. Although I enjoyed meeting Suzy and her family, death brushed my shoulder, an intimation of mortality, as if Roberto and I had shared a fleeting hug.

I told Diana that my blind date was not a cozy Sunday brunch with Roberto, but instead a heartfelt wake with his family, making me aware of my own mortality.

"I'm shocked! He had such a charming vitality. This is unbelievable. Don't worry. I tried to find you a *live* man. I won't give up!" she said, coughing repeatedly.

Consoling her, I asked, "How are you feeling?"

"I think I've come down with some kind of cold or flu. All of these late nights have worn me out. Uri just left town for three weeks, so now I'll get some rest. My eyelids are so swollen it looks like I need an eye lift. It's a good thing I'm not giving any guys blow jobs, or I'd never be able to open my mouth up wide enough. Other than that I'm fine. Maybe we'll get together in a week or two. But as long as I look great for my birthday — that's all that matters."

"What do you want to do to celebrate?" I queried.

"Not think about turning 60 and being a grandmother. Get my swollen eyes down and my libido up," she joked.

I said goodbye to Diana, still thinking about my late date. First dates should be brimming with possibility…not fatality. I needed a date with a good EKG…and a pulse!

9. Beauty By the Lb.
🝆🝆🝆

Later that evening, I went to see Julia appearing as a lingerie model in a National Association of Fat Americans (NAFA) fashion show.

Bright lights, flash bulbs, lightning bolts of frenetic energy filled the room. A packed house with enthusiastic men and women eagerly watched the models take the runway stage. Each voluptuous vixen, more provocative, happy, and steamily sexy than the last, fearlessly strutted the runway in skimpy, lacy undergarments. The crowd cheered as if each had scored a touchdown at a football game. Every beautiful model, her double-D's jiggling as she strode, gloriously feminine, was a glamorous waterfall of fleshy female pride. Screw you, Kate Moss! Victoria, this was the real secret. These were womanly women, in corsets and garter belts, all smoking with mature sexuality, while all of your boy-shorts-wearing girls were really stick-figured pseudo-boys, gussying up for immature man-children.

Julia, her megawatt smile, was striding down the catwalk, her buoyant breasts bobbing in a pink teddy and peignoir. I applauded loudly, cheering. She eyed me, flipped her hair back, and winked. I watched the predominantly male audience, men of different ages, sizes, and shapes, smoldering with sexual heat and desire — hot for these women in these outfits — or out of them — as soon as possible.

For the show's finale, the plus-sized models arrived in a line, all in floor length black silk robes. They opened the robes, revealing a variety of black lace panties and bras. Then they all removed their robes simultaneously, took their bows, and strode off the stage, dragging their robes behind them, a cavalcade of femme fatales, victoriously marching back to the wonderland of Amazon princesses.

Later that evening over martinis, I asked Julia, "You enjoy strutting on a stage in your underwear?"

"All those eyes on me," she cooed, sipping her drink. "It's a fabulous feeling." Dressed in black pants, jacket, a silk bustier with baby pink accents and white lace trim and still in full make-up, hair curled and bouffant, she was as sexy as any movie star.

"And the men cheer!" she smiled. "I was tingling from the admiration."

"I wouldn't have the guts, or the breasts." I ate the olive from my martini.

"It's knowing your audience. Every woman has something about her that's beautiful," she said.

"And this audience tonight? Who are these men?"

"Men who appreciate big, beautiful women," said Julia. "Some are overweight, but most are slim or bodybuilders who get turned on by a fleshy form."

"You see yourself as a fleshy form?" I was surprised.

"There's a goddess inside this vessel! I see myself as lovable, desirable, and silky to the touch." Julia threw her head back and laughed. We clinked glasses. "You should see yourself that way, too. I can get laid whenever I want."

"And who were you with last?" I inquired.

"While I was waiting for this guy from Craigslist to call me back, I met a woman at the Outfest *Film Festival*." She adds, "We're both Ida Lupino fans."

"I wish I could be gender-flexible," I sighed.

"I think you already are. You just need to loosen up a bit. When you see a woman you find attractive, just say 'hello.'" Julia smiled, stroked my arm, and downed the rest of her drink.

I admired Julia's confidence, and the way she dressed and carried herself — quite a provocative package. No wonder she always had a devotee when she wanted one. Could I, a goofy ex-gamine who barely fills an A-cup, find a roster of receptive lovers, too?

"Hello is a brave word right now. I'm feeling invisible in the real world, rejected in the writing world, and without mojo or a live body in Diana's world," I blurted the second Julia put her empty glass down.

"Diana can be a steamroller, Sara. Don't let her get you down," soothed Julia.

"She doesn't get me down. She just flaunts her sexuality in such a way that I feel like I'm a different species."

"You are, dear," Julia replied, "And that's okay. I'll make you feel better about yourself. Remember, I'm your have-a-good-time, get-a-sex-life sponsor. Friday night I'm taking you to a party…a dungeons-and-fantasy party."

"Wasn't that a geek-boy computer game?" I asked.

Julia laughed. "You're thinking Dungeons and Dragons."

"What do you wear to a dungeons-and-fantasy party?"

"I'm wearing black leather pants and a bustier," said Julia.

I gulped. "If I had your body, I'd wear one, too. You wear a bustier out in the world more than anyone I know."

"Everyone should flaunt their assets," Julia said. "For me it's tits. For you, it's wits."

"Okay. I'll polish my wits and see you Friday."

10. Divas Of the Dungeon

Friday night, Julia's dusty Corolla was outside my house at 9 p.m. I slid into her car wearing all black: pants, a long jacket, and a simple, sheer tank top. Julia was in her high-cleavaged glory, with full make-up and lips glossed like a soap opera actress on Univision.

"Are you ready for a fantasy evening?" she asked in a mock Ricardo Montalban accent. We drove for almost an hour, out near the airport, where all the buildings housed U-Hauls, rental cars, or storage units. There was a nondescript, dimly lit building where cars were lining up. "That's it. That's the place."

We parked. The couple walking alongside us looked like corporate office workers who'd arrived straight from their jobs (except for the fact that he had a leather dog collar around his neck and she was holding the chain, walking him to the club). At the doorway stood a woman who looked like Vampira and another dressed in a Catholic school girl's uniform with a thigh-high red plaid skirt.

I exhaled as we entered, thinking I'd be the squarest, most uptight woman there. We were escorted down a long entrance hall by a security hostess dressed in a slinky black jumpsuit á là James Bond's girlfriend. Another door opened…into the party.

Some party. It was a cavernous room that was probably a storage facility during daylight hours, with décor resembling a church basement. Wood-paneled walls provided a backdrop for cheap folding chairs, card tables, and a bar that was merely two tables covered by a paper cloth and offering beers and hard liquor.

Every former 6th-grade geek, freak, misfit, and outsider was dressed up in their best fetish finery. Men were either emaciated or rotund — and leering, more than looking, at the women.

Yes, the women. Where do you shop for freak-show clothes like these? There were two platinum blondes with identical short, spiky haircuts wearing matching black leather mini-skirts and shiny red patent-leather bustiers, pushing basketball-sized breasts skyward. They took turns sitting on each other's laps while they alternately kissed and warmly greeted everyone who sat at their table. Body piercings were everywhere. The most beautiful women in the room were transvestites.

I learned that latex brings out the best curves in everyone. I scoped out the patrons as my eyes ricocheted around the room. The cornucopia of couples was mesmerizing. It was like a car accident — I couldn't look away, repulsed and attracted all at once. The air was heavy with smarmy sexuality.

Feeling like a sexual tourist, I was reminded of the bar I'd visited with Beth. If the gay bar was Paris, this was Amsterdam. Then I found the roadmap for our vacation from "sex as we've known it." I picked up a brochure from a stack on the corner of the card table and read:

"Club DV8 has the nation's largest, most elegant, and best-equipped dungeon. (I'd hate to think we were going to an inferior dungeon; you know how dungeons can be.) *Fully air-conditioned and heated, cleaned daily* (let's hope so), *and filled with state-of-the-art equipment.* (It's so bothersome to use 20th century flogging equipment.) *We have a total of seven complete theme rooms and dungeons in 7,000 square feet plus a 2,500-square-foot social area complete with stage and lighting. Bondage, Spanking, Slave Training,* (what's graduation like?), *Tickling, Role Playing, Wax, Fire & Ice, Foot Worship, Electrical Play, Role Play, Wrestling, Feminization, English Caning* (I don't think that's chair-making.), *Domestic Discipline, Nipple Torture, Suspensions, Flogging, and so much more."* (What's left, fondue frolic?)

I tried not to stare as we ventured to theme rooms where people engaged in their role-playing pleasures. Voyeurism was highly encouraged and seemed to be the preference of the gaggle of geek boys who arrived without female companionship. In one room, I counted 35 people watching as a man was shackled to a wooden stake and then flogged by the woman who'd accompanied him.

I was intrigued, repulsed, and mesmerized by the circus of scenarios that seemed more theatrical than sexual. I got a weird thrill out of being this close to couples touching and sharing licentious energy, making me feel that I was having a second-hand sexual moment, anonymous and in a small crowd. It felt like watching the making of a porno film.

Excited and uneasy, I held on to Julia's arm as we walked from one "theme room" to another, an X-rated Disneyland. Others walked past us, smiling and eyeing Julia as if she were alone. Meanwhile, she and I found all seven rooms: a classroom with old school wooden desks where students were bent over their desks while teachers spanked them with rulers. Next, a boudoir filled with large-size evening gowns, where three large men were whooping it up, laughing, and admiring themselves in Mae West style, the belles of the 1890s-style gowns, each exclaiming over the other's necklaces and feather boas. Another room with a rack and various shackles was very crowded. We perched on the side of a leather massage table and watched couples spank one another. Some brought their own toys and a bag of tricks. Others borrowed from the selection we'd seen in the "goody room" on our way in.

Watching the pain and pleasure at first was titillating. But with each repetitive slap and every tightening turn of the rack and subsequent flogging, the thrilling sensation dulled; Julia and I both started squirming, itching to move on. Before we left, we stopped in one more room where everyone was wearing nothing but Saran Wrap; it was the spanking room.

That room got Julia and me thinking. A 30-year-old man was lying face-down on a table, wearing nothing but a diaper. A woman was spanking him; first hard slaps, then soft, then a gentle rub, like a schizophrenic mother. She looked bored. She was obviously paid to do this on an hourly basis. How did I know? This dominatrix was not young, or beautiful, or dressed in a bustier. She was over 50, overweight, and dressed like somebody's dowdy mom.

Finally we saw our demographic: the invisible, mid-life woman. She was here making a living, helping man-children live out their fantasies! "Mommy porn?" I asked Julia, suppressing a giggle. Then, right outside the room, we saw this sign:

Do you want to work in a clean, safe, and 'drama-free' atmosphere? We welcome top-quality dommes with experience. Also, professional switches with experience, and submissives, no experience necessary. Cash paid daily, great working conditions, make your own hours. Here is an opportunity to work in one of the great Dungeons of the World.

"I'd like a drama-free work environment, wouldn't you?" I said, snarkily.

"With your schedule, you could fit in a few spankings a week," she laughed.

"So, you're encouraging me to apply for this?" I questioned, hesitant, although it could open the door for many article ideas as well as expand my sexual imagination in a dark, disturbing way.

"Oh, yes, definitely!" said Julia. "You could probably write about it for your self-help articles. Women's magazines always clamor for articles on sexual specialties. Besides, you can earn $150 an hour."

"Do you know how many beauty tips and hair care hints I have to wax poetic about for $150? I'm writing down the number," I remarked, excitedly. For that rate, working in a dungeon seemed like a spanking good opportunity. Plus, it had the fantasy I could spin into smut stories for high-paying men's magazines. I could postpone thinking about my own sexual dilemmas and focus on my clients.

By the end of the evening, we were experts on the *Dom Den* experience. People were aroused, but never really had sex, as the exchange of fluids was prohibited. They enjoyed the exhibitionism, the voyeurism, and the pain. As I continued to watch, I told myself that I was merely studying up for my job interview (and future articles). Dominatrix for one of the great dungeons of the world? Yeah, that would look good on my résumé.

11. Theater Games
♛ ♛ ♛

"Please don't let me have a hot flash today. I hope I don't have a hot flash today," I prayed into the mirror, reapplying mascara for my dominatrix interview. I thought I'd check this out — as a lark, of course — but I really needed the money. My writing career was becoming unreliable. I enjoyed eating on a regular basis, but hated living on the financial edge. I also wanted this job for the adventure factor that I could parlay into new magazine articles. I drove to the DV8 building where Julia and I had explored the world of dungeons.

At five o'clock in the afternoon, there were only three cars in the parking lot. Otherwise, the windowless building looked either closed or abandoned. I found the entrance and rang the doorbell. A very short Mexican man with a gold hoop earring answered the door. He led me down a hallway to a small dark office. As we walked, I said to myself, *"Welcome to Fantasy Island."*

Arriving at the dark office, he ushered me in, then disappeared like a genie going back into a lamp. There was a simple black desk, four rickety office chairs, and a Styrofoam cup with bite marks on it sitting on the side of the desk. I was greeted by two women who looked like the mother and daughter from an *Ivory Snow* soap commercial gone bad. They resembled one another, both with overgrown bangs and oxidized blonde hair from the exact same bottle.

"Have a seat," said the younger one, sitting back in her chair, putting her feet on the desk, fidgeting, and crossing her legs seconds later. "Have you done improvisation or theater games?"

At first, I thought this was a strange question. Then it all made sense.

"Yes, I have," I said confidently, trying to balance myself on the most wobbly chair in the room. "I did acting as part of a comedy troupe a few years ago."

"Good," the two women said simultaneously, looking at each other, then at me. "You need a sense of humor for this job, too," said the younger.

"Boy, do you ever," said the older.

"Do you provide a uniform?" I asked.

"Black clothes usually work. Whatever you're comfortable in. We have extra high heels and stockings if someone requests them," the older one added.

"Could you tell me a little bit about the job?"

"It's using your theater experience, being different characters, and role playing," the older one told me. "They choose you and you negotiate what you will and will not feel comfortable doing. The two of you agree on a "safe" word. You engage in your "play" together. If someone wants to stop the experience for any reason, you say the safe word and playtime stops."

I nodded agreeably, taking it all in. "Compensation?"

"You get paid per session, every time someone chooses you. As a beginner, you'll get $150 per client," the younger one explained. "Tips are all yours. And you look like an excellent candidate for our big tippers."

"How so?" According to the "pros" I had the looks of a Dom Den worker?

"I think you'll have staying power," said the older one, while examining her manicure. "Too many girls don't have your sturdiness."

"Sturdiness?" I asked.

"She means a bigger, fleshier behind can take a lot of spanking. Too many girls said this job was a pain in the ass. They get too sore, too many bruises — and they quit," the younger one explained. "Not you. You're strong. I can tell by looking at you that you can take a beating and keep coming back for more."

Was that a compliment? I've never had an interview where the employer had this much confidence in me. Elated that my fleshy ass won them over, I asked, "What else do I need to do?"

"Come back Thursday night around 7 p.m. Wear something black and sexy. We'll see how it goes," said the older one.

Since they thought I was bankable and spank able, I returned Thursday, hopeful, in a black outfit Julia had picked out: push-up bra, stretchy pants, comfortable flat-heeled boots (for all that standing), and a sheer black button-down blouse I wore open, as a jacket.

There were three other women there; a blonde, a brunette, and a tall coffee-skinned beauty, all dressed in black, reading magazines. I sat with them and read magazines, too. After 45 minutes, a curtain parted. A balding middle-aged man with a sweaty upper lip was escorted into the room by the younger blonde from my interview. He smiled at me first, before noticing anyone else. I smiled back, remembering the mirror game from improv class. I noticed he was wearing a cheap belt and well-worn shoes. The other women smiled at him too. The brunette gushed and jiggled her breasts. He chose the blonde. They exited together. The curtain closed.

A half hour later, the curtain parted again. A handsome 20-something with chic beard stubble, who looked like a highly successful ad exec, entered. He smelled freshly bathed and was wearing a buttery soft leather jacket. I really wanted him to pick me — then I might have a fantasy too. He winked at me. My heart pounded with the certainty that I'd be spanking him momentarily. He grazed past me, close enough for me to smell his musky cologne. My body warmed with anticipation. Before I could take another breath, he'd taken the hand of the coffee-skinned woman. They left, closing the curtains.

Within the next two hours, each of the three was chosen. Not me. By midnight, they were all chosen twice; I read through all the magazines and was not picked at all. Apparently my sturdiness was not helpful in the selection process. They said my ass would be an asset, not a deterrent. Or, I wondered, did the clients notice my double chin? Were they just in the mood for a blonde or coffee-skinned beauty? Maybe cinnamon just wasn't the flavor of the evening.

I felt old, overlooked — and invisible. I wanted to believe it was just beginner's bad luck. So, of course, I went back the next night. It was a replay of the first. Man after man looked me over, looked away, and chose someone else. I thought of offering a "newbie special" to a guy in black leather pants who looked like Anderson Cooper. When another guy who resembled David Duchovny showed up, I aggressively elbowed my way in front of the blonde, spanked my own ass — twice, cocked my head to the side, and winked. But I ended up looking like a deranged wind-up doll. Even the Marquis de Sade would have found me needy. No one picked me. It was fifth-grade baseball all over again. Only now I'd squeezed my tits into a bustier and driven 20 miles to be rejected. I felt self-esteem draining out of my body like sand in an hourglass. For someone who was supposed to do the spanking, I felt too beat up inside to continue.

So much for fantasy. I went home — knowing I would never go back. Now I could add undesired dominatrix to my list of disappointments/failures.

That night I took a long bath, hoping to wash away the failed sex worker experience. As I soaked, I obsessively reviewed my sexual history since age 32: over 300 sexless dating encounters, and no spankings either! Whenever I left the house in search of love, lust, or even a cheap imitation of something in between — nothing happened. Zip. Nothing was ever unzipped. No zipper was even fumbled with. Girl got no game. Was I the mistress of misfortune? The victim of vaginal neglect? Did I have the vibes of a born-again virgin? What was wrong with me? Was it me? Was there any way I could blame someone else? Yet in spite of self-doubt, I was determined to hope. I tried not to wear my disappointed desolate heart on my sleeve, but it stuck out like a tattered slip creeping out from the hem of my party dress.

The men I liked were married, gay, or moving out of town. I told myself it was okay that man after man did not provide a love connection — because I was just researching for articles. Yeah — and Hugh Hefner slept with all of those bunnies for the greater good of *Playboy* magazine.

Operation 'just enjoy yourself' — my new attitude for the next half century — was off to a rocky start. I finally left the house for groceries (Lean Cuisine was on sale). In the produce line, an elderly couple strolled past me, arm in arm, talking, delighting in each other's company. Their laughter was a bit unexpected, but certainly pleasant. At one point, they stopped and he kissed her forehead before the giggling began again.

"I want that. I want what they have," I said to myself. "I don't want to be alone when I'm older. I want someone to laugh and stroll with." My eyes followed them throughout the store, envious. How and where would I find someone who could stir those cheerful feelings? It's not like I could pick it up at the supermarket with my Carb-Master Yogurt and Hungry Girl Yam Noodles. But now I had a clearer picture of what it looked like. I'd heard of people who met their mate in a checkout line. But I thought I'd probably have to make a bigger effort to meet people, like go on a date. That's the advice I offered thousands of women in my helpful articles. You'd think I never read a word I ever wrote. Solving other people's problems was the easy part of my life. Helping myself was too challenging. "Lower your expectations" was the new mantra from my birthday intervention. I tried to heed it.

Recuperating and recoiling from my "Dominatrix Disaster," I knew I could count on Diana for brunch and mimosa wisdom. We met for lunch at an outdoor café in Venice, on the beach, overlooking the ocean. We had a corner table, positioned to observe young couples strolling in arm and arm, hair still wet from the shower, no doubt after spending a romantic night and morning.

"I wake up on Sunday mornings, roll over, and wish someone was there to cuddle and kiss, someone to have breakfast with," I told Diana, awaiting our food. "Me too," she said, finishing her second mimosa. "Then I remember all the machinations I had to go through to get them there — and what a pain in the ass they were while they were there. Now I control relationships; I come and go from their beds, then go home in the morning and make breakfast for my daughter."

"Lila told me, wait until you're older and don't have the drive anymore. You won't want anyone in your bucket seat either." I laughed at the pun.

"You won't want anyone in your car, your home, your bed… I'm glad we have each other." Diana raised her glass for a toast. She caught the waiter's eye as he brought a basket of rolls to our table, and ordered another mimosa.

"I'd like you to meet my most consistently amorous lover: food," I said, diving into the rolls. "Beth said, if you had one special girl, you'd have the best of it all."

Diana said, annoyed, "The lesbian left is campaigning again. You're just feeling disappointed by men. You wear bitterness like a diamond necklace. You're a beautiful woman who has an inner darkness shining through. Change your outlook; don't change your team."

"Beth said I have options and should explore them," I added. "Me as a sexual explorer," I said, pondering. "I like the sound of that. Just call me Lewis and Clark of the labia."

Back at home that night, I checked my email. Another note from Derrick on Facebook: *Happy to hear from you so quickly. Glad you like my daughters. Yes, I have a wife, somewhere here in the house. After 16 years we're more like pals than a passionate couple. I always thought YOU knew what passion was. Sadly I never found out. It's very cold here in Chicago tonight. Stay warm — Derrick.*

A married man in Chicago thinks I'm passionate! What good does that do me? Buoyed by an impossible email flirtation, I remembered I still had an active profile online at *Match.com.* Dating sites made the mating game seem like shopping for goodies from a catalog, with photos and descriptions designed to entice buyers. So I entered my password and shopped a bit.

Here were a few:

Bam-Bam In Search Of Pebbles: If you're a feminine, sexy, intelligent, adventurous woman who loves to have fun and if you appreciate a classy, handsome, sensual, intelligent, successful man with a great sense of humor and all my own hair...then let's chat! I love to travel, especially to Europe. My match is: Classy, feminine, sexy, intelligent, sensual, open to anything, and loves to have fun! Not too tall, not too fat, and not too serious.

Immature but humorous. I kept scrolling, searching and reading. Nice Guy in So Cal "winks" at me…that's when they want to contact you but are too lazy or insecure or shy to compose an email. His profile was lackluster. His photo, hairless and goofy, resembled a kid's toy where you put magnetic hair on the bald guy.

Then I saw the magical one. Gaelic Lord was handsome, and looked like a close personal friend of Robin Hood. He wrote:

I seek intelligence, so if you're pretty or beautiful, that's terrific but not my main focus. If you're smart and can handle yourself in a multitude of situations, that's very sexy. I'm looking for someone who can "Tango," not to tangle with. So please bring your "A" game.

Hmmm. That Tango/tangle bit won me over. So I emailed. We spoke — a few times the following day, since he worked at home too. He said he wanted to meet but kept putting it off. I didn't know what to make of the postponing business except he surmised I wasn't likely to shag him in the first 20 minutes. Actually, if he was juggling one or two candidates, I was better off having him get through them before he met me. With any luck, THEY will have shagged him in the first 20 minutes, and then he'd be "free" to appreciate me. This online dating thing was quite competitive.

Just out of curiosity, I redefined my search to women aged 43 to 60. There were half as many, mostly kick ass smart, cynical, and pretty. Each profile sounded more enlightened and life-loving than the last. Their descriptions were crackling with wit, imagination, sparkling sarcasm, and adventure.

Men or women? The question reminded me of the ice cream dilemma of my childhood: vanilla or chocolate? Then, given the choice, I would analyze the differences between the two, because in reality I enjoyed them both. Years later, I discovered the pleasures of a two-scoop cone, where I could indulge in both flavors.

Now, as an adult, and lover of the two-scoop concept, I created a "saved favorites" file — I revisited all the men and women I found interesting and "saved" them for later. After reviewing my selections, I realized I'd saved an equal amount of men and women. So much for picking a team. I'd write to everyone, and as the *Magic 8 Ball* said, "All shall be revealed."

Lila called the following day to invite me to an art gallery opening.

"The photography is of and by cancer victors and their friends. There might be an angle for you to write about," she suggested.

"Ya think this will cheer me up?" I sniped. "Seeing people's malignancies and near-death experiences will get me over my bitterness? Maybe afterwards we could catch a film. How about the Nuremberg trials?"

"Self-pity eats away like a tumor," Lila gently added. "I'll drive you to a new experience. You'll meet strong, brave people. Cancer is worse than dating disasters. You have a tumor of the spirit. Join me, before it becomes malignant."

Friends think I have it bad — dark and bitter, tumor of the spirit. Yuck. Self-help writer — take no pride in being the driver of the bitter bus. If you do, you'll journey alone.

I needed an attitude makeover. I put on my sweats and jogged for an hour till the endorphins kicked in. Exercise to dispel bad feelings. I wrote about that in last year's article: *12 Ways to Get Over Yourself.*

12. Cancer Victors and Their Friends
〽️〽️〽️

Anywhere Lila the wise invites me, I should go. So, the next evening, I dressed to impress, wearing a black silk Chinese pajama outfit, my hair up in a bun with chopsticks through it, and one special piece of jewelry: an ear cuff that hooked along the entire outer rim of my ear, giving the impression that it was pierced in 10 places.

Lila arrived promptly at 8 p.m. to drive to the gallery opening. Smiling while I opened her car door, as I got in, the chopsticks in my hair got caught in the top of the door, tugging at my head and pulling me back. After I maneuvered out of my near whiplash, I slid into the seat. Composing myself, I mustered a smile. Not a good omen.

We arrived at Bergamot Station, a former train station nestled in a nook of Santa Monica that was home to a series of quaint craft and art galleries. Packed with people, mainly older, single women, I felt intrigued and energized by their presence. It's one thing to be unattached and healthy. I can't imagine the mind/body angst of surviving cancer and seeking a partner too. I wanted to take in their life stories one by one.

Still not convinced I should be here, my eyes scanned people, looking at the edgy, emotion-provoking photos. Their comments and reactions were juicy entertainment. I was caught up in the theater of people experiencing art, sipping champagne; the obligatory actors, celebrities, and hunky guys. But the most interesting and attractive of the partygoers were the women over 50 who'd NOT had cosmetic surgery.

As I studied them around the room, I could only assume from my own eager-to-be-thawed iceberg existence that melting a mid-life woman could have avalanche-like repercussions. I thought they carried themselves with an air of boundless life experience, style, and grace, coupled with a treasure chest full of passion waiting to be unlocked. I felt magnetized to their hidden, untouched selves; the aloof, smiling facades they wore, like Academy Award nominees who didn't go home with an Oscar.

I sensed or maybe I projected parts of myself, envisioning that these were women with full lives and empty beds. Maybe they filled their lives *because* their beds were empty. I mirrored their highs and lows and wanted to reach out and touch them, hug them, and hold them close. Touching — that was the scary part. To me, and like me, most of these women seemed untouched for so long. Would they know where to begin?

Their past experiences and memories were with men in heterosexual relationships. Mine, too. It was clear why this group of women resonated with my friend Lila. In her tearful confessions to me over the years, separate from her cancer, all of her untapped passion and sexuality was on ice for a decade. Her aloof husband turned arctic after her surgery. It seemed criminally wrong.

I knew I had no right to compare myself to cancer victors. They faced life-threatening battles, surgery, and other tangible, painful horrors and losses. In this moment I was grateful Lila brought me here, to relinquish my self-pity. It had kept me from being present in affectionate moments and left me laughing at myself because my wants seemed unreachable and unquenchable. Would I ever get close, really close, to anyone ever again, or discover the emotional intimacy I craved whole-heartedly?

If I wanted to melt an untouched woman, I'd treat her the way I'd want to be treated, with a warm smile and lots of eye contact. But how would I approach another woman? Not every woman would be open to the idea — just ask Diana. She recoiled at the thought of two women together.

Sweeping statements about vague scenarios, talking about Virginia Woolf, or examples of other women, was a clumsy beginning. What about a lingering hug for hello or goodbye? These seemed to be feeble attempts to chip away at a female iceberg. Scary undertakings, filled with the risk of rejection. Would the rewards be like having a New Year's celebration with someone wonderful shuddering in your arms?

I observed women in the crowd standing alone, appearing radiant and glowing on the outside, masking inner, untouched yearnings on the inside. I believed they were eager to be thawed and warmed, resigned to the fact that no one would notice them. There were women linked arm-in-arm with men, receptive husbands, and companions. I saw other women wearing wigs, no doubt experiencing the trials of chemotherapy.

Captivated by an eight-piece photo study of women who'd had mastectomies, I stood transfixed in front of the portraits of women cannibalized by cancer, one breast missing, a long slither of a scar where a tear-drop shaped breast and nipple once resided. Another photo, a woman had tattooed a field of flowers over her scar tissue. All of them looked beautiful and strong. I wondered who was hugging them now.

"These are amazing, aren't they?" said a woman next to me. I glanced over and saw a small brunette with almond-shaped eyes and a very glossy mouth. Her breasts were poured into a burgundy leotard, offset by lots of silver jewelry and form-fitting grey slacks.

"Yes, there's so much courage in these portraits," I responded.

"Cancer makes women courageous," she added.

I moved to look directly at her. She was stunning, with the hourglass figure of a young Elizabeth Taylor, no evidence of anything cancer-related, like I'd seen in these portraits. "These women are beautiful."

"Hello, I'm April," she said, extending her hand to me, her bracelets clattering. As our hands touched, her eyes took me in, slowly and deeply, the way a smoker inhales the first puff of a cigarette.

"I'm Sara. What brings you to this event?"

"I'm a healer and a victor," said April. We walked to the champagne table together. The din of other people's conversations faded away.

13. Party Faces
☙ ☙ ☙

The gallery crowd was growing, but all I noticed was April — animated and expressive, talking with her hands. When her jewelry clinked, it sounded like wind chimes.

"I know a lot of people here. Many are cancer survivors," April said, beaming. "I had a bout with ovarian cancer, but I won! Now I help others to keep on winning."

"How do you do that?" I asked.

"I'm a holistic practitioner. I work with clients keeping their lymphatic system healthy." April raised her glass to me, took a sip, and then tilted her head back to swallow, revealing a long, ballerina-like neck. As we toured the gallery together, people nodded and smiled at her. I felt like I was on a dance floor with the prom queen.

Back to reality. I felt someone squeeze my arm. It was Lila.

"I've met a lovely woman. We're continuing our conversation over coffee," she said, beaming. "Want to join us?"

"I'll stay here," I said, thinking out loud. "I can't go now. I've just met an intriguing woman, too."

"Good. I hoped you'd meet new people." She giggled, touching my arm, then walked away.

Back to adoring April.

"Was she your date?" April asked, needing to know.

"She's just a friend."

"Good." April took my arm in hers as we strolled around the gallery. She was heady with charisma, like French perfume, and I was wafting in her essence. Everyone we saw admired her and stopped to chat; doctors, clients, gallery patrons. One woman wearing an elaborate hat kissed April on both cheeks. The two women embraced.

"Sara, Maggie. We saw her photo earlier tonight. She's the woman with the flowers tattooed on her chest," April explained.

To Maggie, I said, "You're so beautiful." I reminded myself that she'd had a double mastectomy. Maggie walked off to join another group of people.

"We've seen everyone and every picture here. What would you like to do now?" April asked.

"I have no car. Whatever you'd like to do would be fine," I said.

The next thing I knew, we were driving to the beach in April's Jeep. It was midnight. The windows were open; our hair was blowing wildly as we listened to Maria Callas arias from *Madame Butterfly*. The ocean air was revitalizing and

April's zeal was contagious. She parked a block from the beach in Venice. As soon as our feet hit the sand, she whipped off her shoes and ran, feet purposefully pounding into the sand. She grabbed my hand to run with her. When we got to the wet sand, she stopped, raised her hands in the air, and shouted with delight as the waves rushed over her feet. I copied her because the moment felt so right.

A few minutes later, April took a step back and exhaled. "Whew! See, that's energizing your senses," she said. "One of the best parts of being alive."

In that moment, I thought one of the best parts of being alive was being with April.

"Let's go," April said breathlessly. I wasn't sure where we were going, but I eagerly jumped in the car. "Where do you live? I'll drop you off."

I was disappointed that our evening — our adventure — was coming to an end.

After a short drive, we arrived in front of my house. I touched April's shoulder. Her hand warmly stroked the length of my arm. This comforted me. It wasn't an old woman's hand. She was a sensual, energizing healer eager to touch me.

"If I didn't have to see clients on Saturdays, I'd love to see you tomorrow," she said. "Day after? Sunday brunch?"

I nodded. "Yes." We moved towards each other for a friendly hug and polite kiss on the cheek, which became a lip graze, followed by little nibbles. I turned slightly, prompting a full-on passionate kiss. It felt strange to kiss someone and taste *their* lip gloss. But her lips were so soft and inviting, caressing and enveloping mine. Gentle lips, delicate tongue, breath increasing, I felt stirred with excitement and anticipation. Encouraged, she leaned in closer, her ample breasts pressing against mine, as if our clothed nipples wanted to kiss, too. They were warm and stimulating, something I could get used to. I wanted to touch her breast, wanted to know if my touch would excite her, but I held back. Too soon, I thought. Swept up in the thrill of our first kiss, in this moment, I was a giddy 15-year-old. I felt as if I was racing up a 100-story elevator and I'd rocket into the sky once I reached the top.

"I didn't expect that to happen," she said.

"Me, either," I mumbled.

"Did we like it?"

"Did we?" I was uncertain what to say.

"I did," she said.

"Me, too," I responded.

"I hope it happens again," she said as we paused, looking at one another, smiling. "See you Sunday."

Rather than being with some old man or some man-child who wanted me to watch *Star Trek* movies with him, April boldly took me where no man had gone before.

The following morning, I woke up and called Beth. "I kissed a girl last night — and I didn't puke afterwards."

"Excellent progress," Beth said, laughing. "What happens next?"

"Brunch Sunday," I excitedly replied.

"I'm happy for you. Remember what Rodney Dangerfield said: Bisexuality immediately doubles your chances for a date on Saturday night."

14. Brunchin' Babes
🌿🌿🌿

April arrived promptly at 11:30 Sunday morning, as sexy in daylight as she had been on Friday evening. She selected a healthy macrobiotic restaurant, Real Food Daily. I found the name of the restaurant to be humorous because the food was familiar favorites re-created from reconstituted soy products and tofu. The bacon and eggs I ordered were soy, somehow colored and shaped to look like bacon, and scrambled tofu, decked out and seasoned to resemble eggs.

In the restaurant, everywhere I looked I saw two women together, delighting in each other's company. Some were young, some old; some had similar haircuts. Suddenly I was in a women's world. Everyone was happy, chatting with her companion, not like some of the married couples I saw in restaurants for their Sunday night dinners, chewing in stony silence because they'd said everything they could possibly think of during the course of their decades of marriage.

I felt at ease, relaxed, not sure if it had to do with what was unique about April, or if it was just the magnetization of our estrogen. Either way, I chewed on fake bacon and enjoyed the day.

"How was work yesterday?" I asked, biting into seven-grain toast.

"One of my clients was an animator for Disney. She said my treatments spark her creativity. She sees colors racing through her mind during our sessions."

"Wow, your work sounds magical," I marveled.

"I help people work through traumas, and I do transformational healing."

I sipped my coffee and gave April a long look, wondering what transformational healing she would perform on me.

After brunch, we strolled through shops in Larchmont Village, considering British soaps and trying on shoes. We both spotted sale signs at an athletic clothing store. We entered, tried on a few things, and bought matching yoga outfits. We walked arm in arm, carrying our shopping bags to the car.

"You know, there's a yoga studio right down the street," April said. "We could wear our new outfits together for a class. I always have extra mats in my car. Let's go right now."

Her spontaneity was infectious. The next thing I knew, I was in a downward dog pose on one of April's mats, wearing my brand new outfit. I agreed to everything April said from the moment we met, like a teen at a new school, trying to fit in. But in the moment, everything she said sounded right and felt so good.

After class, we both glistened with sweat. April's short hair was matted to her forehead and neck. "Let's go to my place for showers and cocktails," she said. "All this clean living should be balanced with some alcohol."

I agreed. We hopped back in the Jeep and cruised to her place, a modest two-bedroom apartment, feng shui'd throughout. Her second bedroom was a treatment room for clients and contained a massage table covered in a beige flannel sheet. The room was sparse and beige, too. She gave me a plush super-king-sized towel and ushered me off to her bathroom.

In her shower the water pressure was a hard pounding that eased my shoulders and neck. The walls steamed up from the warm water. I found a bottle of Aveda moisturizing shampoo and squeezed some out. As I was massaging it into my hair, I felt another set of hands on my head. I was surprised and delighted. Then I felt the warm heat of April's breasts pressing into my back as she kissed my neck. I turned to face April and greet her soft lips as they eagerly engulfed my own, kissing passionately under the hot water.

The shower dripped hypnotically as April embraced me, first holding close, then standing back and reaching down, between my legs, searching, probing, then finding and frantically teasing the warmest parts of me until I ignited and screamed with pleasure. She bit my neck and as the pleasure intensified, I screamed louder. We locked eyes and then kissed. It was a heart-pounding exhilaration, like I had too much of a double Starbucks cappuccino and the caffeine wanted to pry my chest open. Woozy from the hot water, intoxicated by April's passion, I felt fearless in my nakedness.

With April orchestrating the romantic overtures, all I had to do was follow along — like waltzing backwards with a really graceful dance partner. As participant and voyeur, my hands stroked the sides of April's centerfold-perfect form. Any man would desire her. But she was eager to be here with me. I felt brave kissing her shoulder and caressing her breasts, first with my hand, then my mouth. She arched back, delighted. I moved my hand between her legs, nervous, anxious, and apprehensive, and then I glided my fingers up deep inside her, marveling that she felt so much like me.

Hesitant that I wouldn't know how to please her, I took a deep breath, closed my eyes, and touched her as if I were touching myself. Hot water rained down on us. As she climaxed, strangling my fingers, I felt my earlier orgasm re-tingling through me. We clung to one another, a wilted heap against the shower wall.

April took both of my hands in hers, squeezed them tight, and then held them to her mouth for a kiss. Looking in my eyes, she playfully announced, "Cocktail time."

Wrapped in towels, we uncorked a bottle of chilled chardonnay. She poured two glasses, handing me one. Grabbing the bottle and my free hand, we scampered into the bedroom. The décor was jungle safari. The night tables and dresser were an ornate black and gold, with tusk-like handles on the drawers. I was surprised to see animal prints everywhere — tiger-striped curtains and leopard-print sheets on the giant bed.

April set the glasses and bottle down on the table. She ushered me to the bed, removing my towel, then hers. We fell back on a dozen pillows of all different sizes and animal prints. I wanted to laugh, thinking I was in Cher's lair. April handed me my wine. We clinked glasses and sipped. She dipped her index finger into her goblet and stirred the wine. She traced a droplet of wine down my breast bone to my waist with her finger, then followed the line with her tongue. I did the same to her. When I got to her waist, I saw a scar.

"Scars are a body's history. They make us interesting," I said.

"That's my Caesarian, from the birth of my son."

"Where is he?" I bolted up, thinking he could walk in at any moment.

"Don't worry, he's 30," she said, laughing.

"And?"

"And what?" She stroked my wet hair, adoringly.

"Husband? Other kids?"

"My husband left me for a younger woman. At first, I was devastated. Then I met a woman *younger* than his. She made the pain go away." April turned on her side, away from me, finishing her sentence and glass of wine. She poured more.

I knew she had just revealed something exceedingly intimate and important, but I wasn't sure what to make of it. As I studied her spine and fading tan lines, I felt fascinated by her outlook, her candor, and life experiences — volumes worth. Most men weren't this deep and open — or as cool and intriguing. Why did I think about men whenever I found myself getting close to a woman? Was it the writer in me observing, comparing, and contrasting — or the heterosexual trying to justify being here?

Operation "just enjoy yourself" was moving along smoothly. I leaned back into the safari of pillows, feeling that my afternoon's delight was like being hit by a tidal wave. I closed my eyes. When I opened them again, I realized we'd both fallen asleep, pretzeled together for an hour or two. I stirred, waking April. She ravenously kissed me, climbed on top of me, and devoured every inch of me like the cobra woman befitting the jungle land surroundings.

I'd never felt so relaxed or free before, safe to share all of my nakedness without judgment. I didn't have to think about contraception, or lubrication, or ejaculation. We both liked to go shopping and we wore the same size. So far, in my first day of sex with a woman, I was seeing lots of advantages — and I was liking it! Did I ever think I could be with a woman? I could be with *this* woman!

I sat at my desk on Monday morning, drinking a double espresso iced coffee, wondering how I could parlay my new discoveries and experiences into articles for the women's magazines I wrote for. Truth was, the entire women's magazine market was hetero-centric. Every ad, from mascara to Mustangs, sells things to help women entice men. All the articles, too. No one wants to read *Sex Tips With Other Girls* — at least, no one wants to admit it.

I called Beth to tell her about my explorations, knowing she would delight in my discoveries. Beth was away for the weekend with her husband Jeff on a "Tantra for Couples" weekend. When they returned, she and I met for coffee.

"I'm confused," I mused. "I need a flow chart for your sexuality. I thought you were mad for the muff."

"Muff is still my mission, my passion. But I am trying to make my marriage work. I have kids."

"I think I have a girlfriend," I smiled.

"Dish!" Beth listened eagerly.

"She's older, wiser, and undergoing hormone replacement therapy, which gives her the libido of a teenage boy."

"I'm jealous. I want that, too." Beth replied. "Lucky you."

"Exhausted me." I said, raising the cup to my lips, hoping for a caffeine jolt.

"Are you happy?" Beth asked.

"The thrill of the new is exciting. I'm not quite sure what to make of it. I feel more lust and adventure than anything else. I can't tell the others. You're my guide in the lesbian labyrinth."

"You'll be fine," Beth assured me. "Will there be a repeat performance?"

"I hope so," I said, smiling.

15. Lavender Visions
☙ ☙ ☙

I had four more dates with April. They were all pretty similar: dinner, wine, and bed. Each time, I felt more comfortable kissing and touching her — and responding to her exploration of my body. Without fail, though, whenever we were intimate, her stroking some part of me, stirring my pleasure, I thought about what this moment would be like if a man were touching me, feeling his hairy chest rubbing up against my nipples or his hard cock inside me instead of April's skillful fingers.

The night I made dinner for April at my place, she arrived bearing flowers, smile brimming with enthusiasm, rimmed with boysenberry lip gloss. When she kissed me at the door I was glad I'd turned everything off on the stove and oven. As the lip lock leaned into one another, we were pelvis-to-pelvis too, as she pressed me against the wall, her mouth devouring my neck and ears, a passionate hungering that made me want to postpone the planned meal while I relished being her main course. April's passion and devotion brightened my spirits and soothed my inner sadness. I glowed. Finally, I was free to uncork the wine and serve the dinner I'd cooked.

While sipping, April surveyed my living room, intrigued to see all of the books I'd collected. She wanted to know the names of everyone in the photos on the mantle, and anecdotes about them: mother, father, grandfather. She especially liked hearing about my quirky grandfather, who always slept with socks on, afraid he'd catch a head cold in his exposed big toes. After telling of Grandpa, I said, "Tell me about your grandparents."

Hoping she'd serve up a slice of her own history, instead, she spied a wooden box next to the photos, "This is lovely. Tell me about this." She sipped again, skirting her own reveal.

"I bought that on a trip to Italy," I explained. "Ten days with three friends: museums, wine, and shoes. I was able to write off the trip thanks to an article about Italian wines, another one on *"What to pack for 10 days in Europe,"* and *"Everything you always wanted to know about olive oil."*

April laughed, slow, throaty, and sexy. I wanted to drink her in like an intoxicating cocktail. "See my bracelet?" she pointed to a thin turquoise bangle dangling on her delicate wrist. "This is from Italy too. It would be so delicious if we could go there together…and drink in the beauty." She raised her glass to me, then to her lips for a big swallow. "You are my glorious beauty," she raised her glass to me again.

And for the first time, I felt beautiful in her eyes. Dessert was chocolate mousse. I served it in long-stemmed wine glasses with parfait spoons. We sat on the couch together, entwined, feeding each other, immersed in the sweetness of the evening. On this night I thought of no one else, just the magic we created together.

"Wouldn't it be nice if we could do this all the time…you know, live together?" she said, all girlish and idealistic.

I sat up and disengaged from our cozy, mellow entwinement, "Do you really think we know each other well enough or long enough to think about that?" I said, serious about the question.

"I was being wishful, and idealistic. I've been seduced by your mousse!" She leaned into me for a passionate kiss. I melted into her sensuality, lost in time, place, novelty, and sensibility, drenched in desirability. After so many dates with men who had now become nameless and faceless to me for their indifference or rejection of me — here and now I was a hot commodity! I slurped up every self-esteem-quenching moment of passion without a thought for next week or next year — just gorging on the heat of the moment and how it filled my hungry heart and heated my uber-rejected, underappreciated self.

By the end of that evening I did not learn anything new about April's past or family. She avoided my questions about them. In the morning I woke up with three hickeys near my navel and bite marks on my left thigh. Overall, I felt contented.

Then there was the night April invited me to her client's wedding at a mansion in Malibu. When she arrived to pick me up, April was wearing form-fitting silk pants and a tight turquoise wrap top that oozed cleavage and sexuality. If I didn't know better I'd think she was dressed purposefully provocatively to pick up new hot prospects. I was surprised, since I was certain it was going to be an all-female lesbian wedding.

When we walked into the wedding, I saw a living room with French doors that opened to a well-appointed backyard. It was half filled with attractive straight men our age, dressed in tuxedoes. They all smiled warmly and leeringly at April and her eye-catching breasts. She nodded knowingly at their admiring glances. The more that men noticed and smiled at her, the tighter she held to me as if to say, "You want me? See who I'm with? I don't need a dick. I don't need men."

April drank lots of champagne that night, hardly speaking to any of the women in the room. Instead she flirted with the handsomest of men, rubbing up against them in conversation, touching and fingering the studs on their crisp tuxedo shirts, as if she wanted more from them. But why here and now, and why if she was with me?

One man started to follow her around the room, first with his eyes, then striding to be just a few feet away from her wherever she was. As soon as she became aware of his pursuit, she grabbed my arm and dragged me upstairs to the master bedroom, and then into the room's gigantic walk-in closet.

Bothered by April's behavior, I was glad she took me away from the party to give me a tour of the house. I liked her best when we were alone together. Venturing into the off-limits part of the house was exhilarating. After turning on a tiny light in the closet, I saw a beige suede settee with animal print pillows. The rack behind it held Chanel suits, evening gowns, and other finery. Before I could examine the garments, April grabbed my arm and kissed me hard on the mouth, then roughly squeezed my breasts, while her hand speedily raced up my skirt, tugging at my panties.

"Where's the fire?" I whispered, laughing.

We both giggled, and then paused as we heard footsteps climbing the stairs. This didn't stop her. Instead, it fueled her ravenous behavior as she practically ripped my panties off, tongue diving deep inside me. The footsteps got faster, louder, closer. The room was hotter and so were we, heaving and moaning.

Then I felt a heavy breathing at the closet doorway, followed by a gasp. April turned for a second, glancing at the shadowy male figure lurking in the doorway.

"Go away. I'm with my girlfriend. We don't need a man. Go back downstairs."

She resumed pleasuring me. I'd never had someone else watching me while I was being made love to. The moment heightened my excitement. April was on fire too, her tongue darting to new places in unique ways. I felt her heart pounding on my thigh.

The man in the shadows stared at us another minute, then spun on his heel and left. As soon as the sound of his footsteps faded, so did April's passion. I was on the edge of orgasm — then, I no longer felt her tongue, or her touch. I was confused.

"Let's go back to the wedding," she whispered. "The music and dancing should be starting soon."

"A few more minutes. I'm almost done," I said, stroking her hand, hoping my big O moment was forthcoming.

"Let's finish later," she insisted. "Dance now, make love all night long."

I wondered if her performance was part of the evening's entertainment for her. Was it to tease him? A dare for me? Excitement for herself? A perverse game of cat and mouse and who gets the pussy? Or was she just drunk?

This exhibitionist behavior was scintillating, disturbing, exhausting, and might somehow bite me in the ass someday. But until then, it could be a joyous jungle-printed merry-go-round. As the champagne went to my head, I tossed off those thoughts. We spent the rest of the evening on the dance floor. Maybe this was the prom night I'd always wanted.

In the car on the way home I was outwardly silent. But inside, I rehearsed the conversation I was afraid to speak, filled with anger, frustration, and feelings of powerlessness. As the car sped along the coast highway, I looked out at the water, the waves, and how it reminded me of our first night together — crashing waves and sultry breezes on the sand — never dull, always on the edge of rocky.

April broke the silence, inquiring, "How are you, dear?"

"What happened in the closet?" I blurted. "Power? Exhibitionism? Control?"

April laughed her throaty laugh again. This time it wasn't sexy, but menacing instead. We clearly lusted after one another. But could I trust her?

I was conflicted. I knew I didn't want to be alone, but did I really want April? Was our time together a budding relationship? Was it a celebration of my newly awakened sexuality? Or was it my consolation prize for not being with a man? Stop thinking and just enjoy yourself, was the last thing my inner voice said before zoning out on the view from the car window.

The following night, each of us pushing a giant shopping cart, Beth and I navigated the warehouse aisles of COSTCO.

"She was doing you there in the closet and then just stopped," Beth exclaimed. "That's more mean than kinky. Did you tell her you were angry?"

"I tried to express myself," I said meekly. "But I think it sounded more like a self-help quiz than my feelings," I said while loading my cart with vast quantities of canned goods.

"You didn't tell her how you really felt," said Beth. "You can't have an honest relationship if you're unable to talk about things."

"I had a husband who lied about everything from who he was fucking to whether or not he ate an ice cream sandwich while walking the dog. Do I even know what an honest relationship looks like?" I asked, with concern and sincerity. "I don't think you have an honest relationship with Jeff."

"Ya know, it's a problem," Beth responded.

"April avoids talking about herself, as if there is a veil of mystery separating us."

"Maybe you like that about her. Avoiding emotional exploration has its appeal."

"Am I an unfocused lesbian?" I asked my favorite sexual juggler, hoping she would help me navigate my uncharted explorations. "When I'm intimate with April, I always think about how it would feel if I were having sex with a man."

"You're trying to sort out too much of your old dirty laundry," Beth explained. "Just forget about boxer shorts for a while. Try to focus and be in the moment."

"She makes me feel great. But I know how I am. I sit in a restaurant with a delicious plate of food in front of me while my eyes eagerly follow a waiter carrying a different, amazing dish."

"I've seen you do that," Beth said.

"She's a hot dish. But sometimes I wish April had a penis," I whispered.

Beth laughed girlishly. "That's what makes being with a woman so interesting. She can get one…or more."

Later in the day, we were sitting on Beth's living room couch. Her husband Jeff was outside mowing the lawn. The hum of his lawnmower reminded me of my old vibrator, the one I'd stopped using since I met April.

"Does thinking about dick make me a hetero on holiday?" I asked.

"Don't think about labels. Think about what makes you happy," Beth implored. "That's the lesson I've been learning lately. Jeff and I went to that Tantra weekend, did intimacy exercises, learned a lot, and got closer."

"What happens at a Tantra weekend?" I asked.

"You spend a lot of time in your underwear or naked, facing each other, cross-legged, gazing endlessly into each other's eyes. You learn listening skills. They call it mirroring. Jeff said something and I repeated what I heard. Then the skills counselors help you see if you are correct or not. You learn to reflect back the love that was mirrored in your partner."

"Was it successful?"

"When we first got back from the weekend, we did our exercises every night. We were closer than when we were first married. Before that weekend I was worried. I thought I had nothing left for him. I felt dried up inside. When we're talking in that face-to-face clinch, my body just starts humming. I become so turned on! I'd been trapped in this peri-menopausal mayhem. Now, my passion and sexuality are back."

"Congratulations," I said. "I don't think Hallmark makes a card for that."

"Don't get too happy for me. I see my own problems more clearly," Beth said.

"What problems?"

"I still want intimacy with a woman," Beth replied. "Sometimes Jeff is cool about it. Other times, he's uncomfortable."

"What are you going to do?"

Beth stood and walked to the nearby desk, picked up a pamphlet, and handed it to me: *Lavender Visions*.

"You know how I love a weekend workshop. Last weekend was a Lavender Visions weekend," she said. "It's a support group for married, bisexual women. There were 18 of us there from all over the U.S. and Canada. All the women were beautiful — and accessorized. It was nice to learn that I'm not alone."

"What did Jeff say about this?"

"He encouraged me to go. Since it was all married women, he knew they'd bolster my staying married and offer solutions for juggling the two sides of me."

Listening to Beth, I thought about myself: no husband, no kids, and no strong attachments to anyone, really. She was juggling two sides; I didn't even have one.

Beth continued, "Marriage vows were written before people lived long lives — or acknowledged their lesbianism. All of the women at the workshop said they're honest with their husbands. They have understanding and open relationships. They all seek out sex with women but don't want to hurt their best friend — their husband — or leave their marriage."

Beth brimmed with emotion, so I hugged her. I was happy she had found a support group to sustain her. I really was. But I couldn't help feeling a tiny sting of jealousy. I saw myself as a party of one, a pot without a cover, a player without a team. Was I an ambivi-sexual? I was a woman without a support group. I had to find someone to mirror my feelings.

16. The Ambivi-Sexual
ᴥ ᴥ ᴥ

Pleased I was starting to have a sex life, not sure if it was really a burgeoning love life. Whenever I felt confused about my sexuality, which happened at least daily these days, I remembered that Julia really was my touchstone in the single world. For all of her experimentation and wacky encounters, she was alone. Like me. On Tuesday night, I cooked dinner for us, with a great bottle of Cabernet and a low-cal chocolate dessert. My goal: deep-dish brain-picking.

"Who do you see yourself within five years?" I asked, pouring a second glass of wine for each of us.

"With a woman," Julia replied.

"Are you sure?"

"Most certainly," she said, caressing the wine goblet with confidence. "Let me ask you — men or women, who do you trust more?"

The table was turned; now my brain was being picked. "Women?" I said with uncertainty.

"Who do you feel more comfortable being naked with?"

My mind replayed whatever past experiences it could find, "Women?"

"Really?" Julia's voice lilted upward, in a way that always made me smile.

"There's a self-sufficient ease that mid-life women have. Their figures resemble Renaissance paintings. Lush nude forms, in the French countryside. Their bodies say, 'This is who I am. Take it or leave it.' If an invisible woman dances naked, and no one sees her, is she any less beautiful? They are incredibly unhurried and glowing."

"Who do you have better sex with?" Julia asked.

We both laughed, knowing I had to stumble through my memories, reaching back to my 20s and 30s for happy recollections and comparisons.

"Wait," I said. "I need an extra minute. I'm not quite in this century yet. My brain is still processing." After a brief pause, I admitted, "Men!"

Julia laughed. "There are challenges in any relationship. But I believe women make better partners," she explained. "They're more focused on maintaining relationships and nesting, loving feelings."

"Those feelings and emotions can make women more moody and erratic."

"And erotic," Julia added with a sweet giggle. "They understand how your engine runs, what makes it purr."

"Single men want sex, with anyone they can find," I said. "They take their taste, lick their lips, and move on. I feel like I'm an appetizer at a cocktail party."

"I think you're the bitter turnip on the appetizer tray," replied Julia.

"I guess I'm angrier at men than I thought I was," I confessed.

"Yet you defend them, like they're the only dish on the menu."

"They've been the main course on MY menu," I said.

"And you've been love-starved for years!" Julia pointed out.

"I never felt strong enough to deal with the social stigma of being with a woman," I explained. "Most of my world is straight — or straight-minded."

"Your friends love you and will cheer for your happiness, no matter who you're with," she said.

"I don't think Diana is a lesbian cheerleader," I offered.

"She's one person," Julia said. "Besides, whenever she's in a relationship, you never hear from her. You need to do more sampling, meet more women, taste different experiences," Julia explained. "Sex with one woman does not make you a lesbian. You can't judge your entire sexuality by one partner. That's so prehistoric and dull."

"What about monogamy?"

"It's easy to be monogamous once you've gotten a lay of the land, so to speak. Monogamy without other experiences is monotony." She laughed at her own joke.

"That's my problem?" I asked, eager for resolution.

"Be open to new experiences. Say hello to people you see on the street. Smile at total strangers. Open yourself up to the world and the answers will come to you."

Two days later, I soaked in a bubble bath, primping for a date with April — and I was still thinking about men, angry that I felt ignored by them.

I remembered walking down the street, painfully aware that as a mid-life woman I was invisible to almost any man who passed me. Men didn't even glance up and then look away — they *never* turned their heads towards me in the first place, like I was not even worth a peek, as if I weren't there. These feelings were confirmed by the world of Internet dating, where most men, no matter what their age, listed themselves as only interested in women up to 44 years old. When a friend recently turned 46 and wanted to date online, I told her the age-range factoid and instructed her to "pick an age from 40 to 44, then just do the math when asked questions about your childhood."

Why were confident, self-assured women at their sexual peak invisible, ignored, and undesired on the American landscape? I'd just seen the film *Door in the Floor* at a revival house. When mid-life beauties Kim Basinger and Mimi Rogers had sensual nude scenes, the audience gasped with the same surprise and amazement as they did viewing the special effects moments from a *Star Wars* film.

I believe a mid-life woman is like a classic car, a fine wine, or an imported cigar. The engine purrs, with a complex taste and a smooth, relaxing smoke. What did men want? Naïve girls they could control? Oh, how I wished a sharp, insightful man, who could appreciate the passion, depth, and beauty of a seasoned, sensual woman, would smile at me on the street and offer a friendly *"Hello."*

As I got out of the tub and toweled off, I thought, "If only I could turn away from the need for male approval and acceptance, I'd love life more and feel better about myself. I dated men and they were hurtful and disappointing. Yet I date a woman now — and all I think about is dick. Would a chick with a dick make me happy?"

That night, as if reading my mind, April brought a treasure chest of sex toys into bed. First, she tickled my naked torso with a feather. I didn't care for it. Then we rubbed each other with chocolate-scented massage oils. Not only did they taste like chocolate, there was a heat-like sensation on my skin that turned me on. This was more like it — my two favorite pleasures, food and sex, combined! Finally, she rummaged through the box and pulled out a strap-on dildo.

In this moment, I heard Julia's voice say, "Open yourself to the world and the answers will come to you."

Fully aroused and engaged, tingling with anticipation, thinking this escapade would answer some of my questions and concerns, I kissed April passionately, fondling her breasts. She stroked my skin: arms, legs, and back. I felt cared for and at ease, ready for anything. We both fumbled with the fasteners on the dildo harness. April fit it to herself and positioned the life-like penis so it seemed to belong to her body. I swiftly slid down the pillows on my back, trying not to seem too eager for penetration. She paused and turned away. I took a deep breath, my insecurity getting the better of me. To my relief, April reached into her night table for a half-empty tube of lubricant. She'd obviously done this quite a few times before.

With ballerina-like grace, April straddled me. First she probed deep inside me with her fingers, making sure I was wet and ready. With the other hand, she lubricated our new friend. When everyone was hot, wet, and ready, the dildo dance began.

At first, penetration was uncomfortable, then familiar. As April thrusted inside me, I admired her firm torso, jiggling breasts, and delighted smile. She was enjoying this as much as I was. A gorgeous, adoring woman was making love to me — and I felt filled up inside. I had no wants or thoughts of men!

I wet my fingers with my tongue and touched them to April's nipples, which hardened in seconds. I grabbed her entire breast, squeezing in rhythm with her thrusting inside me. Seconds later, we both came, hard. She collapsed on top of me and I held her close. Her heart pounded against mine. Now that she had fucked me like a man, something inside me felt safe to open my heart to her. I held her tight, as if it would help me hold onto the warmth of loving feelings that were welling up inside me. This was the first moment I thought I was falling in love with April.

Next, April brought out another toy and explained that the strap-on blow job was the ultimate in gender-bending sex theater, because our biggest sex organ was our brain. It's all about desire. The idea, the visual thrill, the feeling of power, and the unique physical sensations all combined to make our motors rev. The person on either side of the dildo was in a position for which no romantic comedy or high school sex-ed had prepared you. At first I was uneasy, but April encouraged me to do some deep yoga breathing — and like a master of meditation, my mind let the weirdness go.

"I like watching my lover's head bob up and down the shaft," April said eagerly, getting into the perverse thrill. While I sucked away, she revisited my wetness with her hand, frantically stroking my clit. I fondled her breasts. We both came hard, again.

As I held April in my arms, spent, satiated, and happy, my mind replayed Julia's question: "Who do you have better sex with: men or women?" I shouted my answer out loud. "April! April!" I hugged her tightly, my ever-opening, happy heart pressing against her body, and we both drifted off into blissful slumber.

17. Color My World
♛ ♛ ♛

I was now keenly aware that April's affection was healing a lifetime of rejection. Her hormone-replacement-derived, over-active libido and sizzling sex-fests in her jungle-printed boudoir were saving me. So I dove into April like she was the Pacific Ocean and I was a long-distance swimmer training for the Olympics. Our weekly romantic evenings became long weekends of unending sensuality.

Sure April seemed manipulative, controlling, and odd at times. There were things I wished I could change — but at the same time, I didn't want to rock the boat. I finally had a sex life and someone who adored me. That's why I had mixed feelings when April invited me to a healing session in her office. From everything I'd heard about her work, I anticipated a full-blown sensory experience, envisioning little paddle boats floating through my veins, floating toxins out of my body. As I pulled into the parking garage under the building, I realized April must be more successful than I'd thought. With a high-rent office walking distance from Rodeo Drive, Saks, and the most expensive stores in town, surely her clientele were paying a pretty penny for the esoteric experience of her healing specialties: lymphatic drainage and chromo therapy.

Entering the office, a receptionist greeted me. All shades of sand and Santa Fe design, there were plush sofas and current magazines in the waiting room. After reading 20 pages of *In-Style*, I was ushered into April's treatment room. There she was, wearing a white cotton lab coat over her low-cut silk blouse and tailored mocha pants. No kiss hello — she was all business, an aloof grown-up in the working world.

"Please remove your clothes, and then get under the blanket on the table, face up," she said seriously, with rehearsed composure. Then she left the room. Usually she likes to watch me undress, I thought. Surprised, I meekly obeyed her directive, sliding under the blanket on the table, face up.

April knocked and re-entered, still serious. Even her voice was impersonal. "How are you today? Any pain or perceived blockages?" she asked.

I knew this must be her standard opening. Somehow I thought my session would be peppered with endearments. But this wasn't a date, I reminded myself.

"My lower back is a little tight."

"Close your eyes and breathe deeply," April replied, touching my forehead as if taking my temperature. Then her hands glided over the blanket along my body as she took an energy assessment. I peeked periodically to see what she was doing. She reached for an instrument on a nearby table. It looked like a wide-toothed comb. "I'm using a guasa. It's an ancient Chinese instrument that stimulates blood flow and circulation and revitalizes the lymph system. Guasa therapy was used to purify, oxygenate, and activate cells. It helps boost your immune system." Uncovering my left arm she proceeded to "comb" it in gentle strokes similar to a massage. The experience felt a little like a girl playing with one of her Barbie dolls. I wanted to laugh — but wondered: if I had an inner giggle, would April be able to detect it?

April was in a trance-like state, tuning into and conducting energy, as if she were internalizing every response my body was giving off. I tried to focus on the sensations I was experiencing. She was working on my right leg, combing, focusing, concentrating. I finally relaxed, closed my eyes, breathed deeply, and tuned into the moment.

My mind raced, as if a series of movies from childhood were being played at high speeds. First, my four-year-old self was on a tricycle, riding, then falling over. Next, I saw myself running bases in a fifth-grade softball game. My mind's eye was bombarded with flashes of color, as if a dozen Jackson Pollack paintings were being shown to me at high speed. I came back to the present and realized April was touching my core chakras, somewhere near my belly. I opened my eyes and saw a Daliesque image: April was there, but I saw a giant beating heart outside of her body, as if the organ had dived out of her chest and was trying to move into mine. I gasped.

It was as if the treatment had taken my senses on a psychedelic trip. My entire self was like two beakers of colored liquid in science class; as the teacher poured one into the other, they combined to become a third color, then bubbled over. I was surging with thoughts and feelings moving faster than I could process them. My mind was exploding with imagery, colors, and ideas. Not a dark image or demon in sight! This was truly an *Alice in Wonderland* experience. After she combed my entire body, April put the guasa back on the table and walked to a cabinet that featured about a dozen square bottles. Each was a different solid color and glowed like gemstones.

"I'm going to finish with some chromo therapy. It's an ancient Egyptian practice, using color to enhance the glandular functions of your body. Each color has a different meaning. I think you need some green today." Removing the emerald-colored bottle from the shelf, she cupped it in her hands as if to warm it. Then she touched my core again. Reaching for my foot and uncovering it, she poured green liquid into the palm of her hand, gently massaging it into the bottom of one foot, then the other.

After rubbing my feet, April recovered them with the blanket. Next she used sweeping motions across me, from head to toe, to clear and release energy. Then she repeated the same motions to cleanse herself.

"Take a few minutes to feel your relaxation. Then dress and go to the waiting room." Spent, she left the room.

I felt as cherished and nurtured as an infant. This was the most tender, loving moment I'd experienced with April. In this time I wasn't her lover, her intimate, or her confidante. She was being a powerful and magnetic healer, giving of herself to her client. I was amazed she had any energy left at the end of a work day.

When I was back in my clothes, April met me in the hallway. I moved to hug her and kiss her cheek, but she resisted. No doubt the white coat was our chaperone.

She smiled. "I hope today was helpful for you," she said. "Call me tonight."

As I walked to the elevator, all my senses were heightened, so much so that even the colors of the celadon hallway and the lighting seemed brighter than when I entered. I'd now experienced "business April" — a serious, professional, magical healer who threw her entire self into renewing her clients and facilitating transformational experiences. She was a master, making everyone she touched feel better — especially me.

Relaxed, renewed, and brimming with creativity, I was raring to go home and write. Yesterday, I turned in stories on *Summer Hair Care Tips* and *How to get Beach-Worthy Thighs*. My current deadline was a relationship piece. The more I dated April, though, the tougher it became to crank out dating-dilemma articles about guys.

Luckily, my memory and imagination were energized by April's body combing. I remembered a summer three years ago when I dated two divorced men. Every other weekend, they both had child custody; to have a consistent social life, I was in two relationships, alternating the weekends they had their kids. This memory certainly filled the bill of "dating dilemmas with guys." I turned in my *Dating Divorced Dads* article, and then took a bubble bath. While soaking, I reflected on the duality and secrecy that was now a part of my daily life. No wonder my sexuality was like a surfer being tossed by waves on the ocean. I earned my bread and butter from writing about dating men. Meanwhile, my biscuits and gravy were about dating a woman.

18. Crashing Waves
🐚🐚🐚

As soon as I toweled off from my bath, I called April. Sounding giddy as a teenager, April said, "Big plans for the weekend. Pack a bag. One of my clients is going out of town for a week. She wants me to house-sit for her in Malibu, right on the water. We'll be beaching in luxury. I'm going there tomorrow. Meet me Friday night."

I hung up the phone and sat back on my couch, pondering. I gave dating tips to hopeful single women about successful relationships with men. I hadn't had a flourishing association with a man in almost a decade — and here I was trysting with an amazing, magical woman, old enough to be somebody's grandmother. It all felt unfamiliar, but pretty delightful!

Friday evening, six o'clock traffic was bumper to bumper on Pacific Coast Highway, the only road to Malibu. I was stressed about the traffic, anxious, and excited, frantically chewing bubble gum, anticipating that my over-sexed cobra woman would serve up sexual adventures beyond my imagination. With the adrenaline of a teen-aged boy, I hoped for a smooth and easy, non-stop sex-a-thon at the beach — more fantasies, but instead of jungle land, a beachy motif.

(Sort of *Beach Blanket Lesbians*, with one of us in the Annette Funicello role.)

Traffic finally thinned out, and so did all of the buildings, stores, and homes. I drove into the rustic part of the beach, checking the directions. I wasn't lost — I was half a mile from my destination. I turned down a narrow, unpaved road. I was here — at a tiny house right on the beach. It looked like paradise.

I parked my car next to April's Jeep, got my bag out of the trunk, and knocked on the door. April answered wearing a sheer black teddy, a sheer black peignoir edged with marabou feathers, black stilettos, and fishnet stockings with garters. She held a pitcher of margaritas.

"Welcome to Malibu," she said, in her sexiest vixen voice.

"This is no grandma," I thought to myself, incredulous that I ever thought of April that way. "Baby, you're hot!" I said to her, wondering how I could transcribe this moment for my straight readers. I entered to April's passionate kisses on my mouth, then neck. Dropping my bag on the floor by the door, still smooching, April waltzed me into the living room and tenderly laid me down on a bear-skin rug.

She quickly undressed me, whispering, "I want you naked."

"You're not naked," I said.

"I may dress you up. We'll see." She poured two glasses. "You must be thirsty from your trip." As April handed me a glass, margarita spilled on the back of her hand. She wiped it on my stomach, then licked it off. (Didn't I write this scenario for *Cosmo* last year as part of my piece, *A Dozen Ways to Make Him Want You More?*)

My senses were revved! I was drinking a perfectly chilled margarita, facing a view of the ocean at sunset, being undressed in anticipation of mind-blowing sex, with someone who had the libido of an 18-year-old boy. This was nirvana.

April climbed on me, hungry, almost animal-like. Her kisses turned to bites, first tingling, then rough. I pulled back.

"Careful, that hurts," I said, wriggling away.

"I want you...close, closer," she said with demanding intensity.

Alarms rang in my head. "I'm right here, baby. Just take a breath. Slow down," I said soothingly. "We have all weekend to be together." I rubbed her back in calming circular motions, trying to ease an over-active child.

"I need you. I want you," she insisted hungrily.

"I'm not going anywhere." I said, disturbed by her urgency. "I wouldn't even find my way back to the road until daylight. I'm here with you — and for you." I moved to kiss her.

April pulled away and moved to sit on the taupe silk couch. "You don't love me the way I need you to love me."

What? I took a deep breath, sat up from the floor, and faced her. "I love you."

"I work all week long," April said, "Giving myself to clients, moving their energy, opening their closed hearts. You've seen how exhausting it is."

"You're great at it, a goddess in what you do."

"I give to everyone. I chose *you* to give to *me*," she explained with great emotion, then looked away.

I moved to sit close to her and touched her cheek to face me. "I love you," I said again. I kissed her forehead. Those words surprised me as I heard them. Did I mean it? Was I really past dating and finally in a relationship — one worth working at? Or was I just struggling to have the weekend run smoothly?

She pulled away and stood. "You'll never love me enough." Her voice sounded demonic. My mind flashed to the night in the closet. On both occasions she was a different person. Was that a character, or a role she was playing — a woman in a faraway place? Was tonight's scene about a peignoir and a beach house? How could I play my part differently?

I leaned my head back on the couch and sighed. I remembered my session in her office and her remote, distant behavior. Yet she touched me and reorganized all the energy and intense feelings swirling inside me. The power of conducting other people's chakras and realigning them was like creating a typhoon at will. No wonder I found her so electrifying. Was this moment a part of her decompressing from work? Or was I experiencing what it's like to be on the receiving end of a hormonal rant? I shook my head and sipped my drink, unsure of my response. April stood, still in stilettos, staring at me. No, Dickens, *this* was the best of times — and worst of times. How do I turn this romantic interlude, suddenly soured, back around?

I could not let her control me. I had to take charge. I stood to bring her back to the couch, firmly reaching for her wrist. She flinched. I grasped her hand, then encircled her waist. "Come closer, let me love you." I gently nibbled her neck. She responded favorably for an instant, then pushed me away, hard. I fell back on the couch.

"What do you want?" I asked, exasperated.

"I want your devotion!" she blurted, throaty and desperate, as if possessed by Norma Desmond.

Kneeling at her feet, hoping this would end the outbursts, I said, "You have it."

April glared at me, yelling, "Not enough!" Grabbing the pitcher, she twirled to find her glass, then sashayed to one of the bedrooms, her peignoir floating behind her.

I moved to follow, but she slammed the door behind her. I heard it lock.

Shocked, I thought, who was this menopausal monster, prettied up like a vixen, spewing venom? Did giving her all to clients make her ravenous to receive? Had it been an overly traumatic week? Was it fatigue, new environs, and high expectations? She'd turned into a bottomless pit of love-starved neediness that could only be satiated by isolating me and sucking me dry — worlds away from the magical healer or sexual dynamo I'd known.

Frightened by her tantrum, I worried about what was in store next. Was she inconsolable, ready for a rant or rage, a night of opera without resolution? Should I knock and try to resolve her concerns? Or just let her be? Maybe we should both get a good night's sleep and start fresh in the morning, I thought, deciding to heed the locked door. I took a breath, got my bag, then found another bedroom. On my way, I admired the view out of every window. I was in a beautiful place with a gorgeous woman — and hopefully, tomorrow morning, April would be herself again.

I found a room where the walls, dressers, and bedding were all pale, beachy colors. Giant seashells decorated the walls. Exhausted, my mouth felt as if it were filled with sand, so I finished my drink and got ready for bed — alone.

Fresh sheets and a firm mattress felt good after a long day of writing, driving, and arguing. Turning out the lights and settling in, my head sank into the pillows. Blankets caressed my chin. I drifted off to sleep, lulled by the sound of the ocean.

Three hours later, I awoke to something that sounded like trash cans being turned over. But it wasn't. The tide came in, waves crashing on the beach, piercingly loud, and so close to the house that I thought water would burst through the windows.

This moment would feel so much less scary if I were holding April — and she was holding me. I got out of bed and walked to her room. The door was still locked. Agitated, I tiptoed back to my room and got back in bed.

I couldn't fall back to sleep. It was as if the ocean were a noisy neighbor holding a block party until dawn. I finally fell asleep around 6:30 a.m., only to be woken by April two hours later as she clattered around in the kitchen.

Out of bed, I brushed my teeth and hair, put on shorts and a shirt, and walked to the kitchen, hoping I'd meet the "old" April. "Good morning. How did you sleep?" I said cheerily, trying to muster every ounce of congeniality my sleep-deprived self could find.

"Shit, everything is shit," she shouted. "Who can sleep in this place? The coffee is shit. I feel like shit."

I moved to comfort her. "If we were together in the same bed last night, we both would have slept better." I kissed her neck. She hesitated. I buried my head there, smooching, tightening my caress around her. April finally calmed. She just needed some warmth, I said to myself, confident I'd soothed her.

She puttered around the kitchen wearing a salmon-colored silk kimono. Beautiful and making breakfast right in front of me, April mixed vitamin powder, soy milk, honey, and fresh fruit into the blender. As the pale concoction whirred in the glass container, I thought of the past night's events. April poured a glass and offered it to me with a warm, girlish smile

— and I chose to erase the evening's outbursts from my mind.

After breakfast I went to my room and called Julia. "Women can be more challenging than men. April has a Hyde side of her Dr. Jekyll that's frightening."

"You told her you love her? Things are past teen-age lust and honeymoon sex. You need to work on growing your relationship," Julia insisted. "Go work."

"Okay, I needed to work harder. Here goes."

April and I put on bathing suits and walked to the beach. As we stepped closer to the ocean, I remembered our first beach kiss, brimming with electricity, shyness, and the thrill of the new. Now, it was different. After last night, seeing April's underbelly of neediness and insanity, I felt cautious and guarded.

We romped on the sand like kids, running into the water, then jumping back out. The waves whooshed back at us — a lot like the way I'd behaved in most relationships before now. Was I afraid of getting close to someone? I needed to believe I was more evolved now, capable of building a lasting rapport.

After a glorious day on the beach, we relaxed on the deck, sharing a bottle of champagne, pate, and crusty olive bread.

April was quiet most of the time, speaking only when the last drops of bubbly hit the glasses.

"You haven't said anything about last night," she began. "There's a lot of male energy in your behavior. I like it."

"What should I say?" I asked, hoping she'd feed me the lines for this play.

"We should talk about our love, our love for each other," April said, insistently grabbing my arm. "Where is our love going?"

Her hand was an annoying clutch, like when Will touched me — an older man's need to hang on to youth, or a vampire's hunger to feed on new blood to stay alive.

"Our love is here right now." I said, barely convincing myself. "Where does it need to go?" In this moment, feeling like a caged animal, I recoiled.

"I n-e-e-d to know your commitment level," she said pointedly. "I need to know about our future. Otherwise, I'll always be holding back, not feeling free to be myself."

I looked at her, perplexed. April was so strong — yet her insecurities signaled a deep neediness. I'd wanted someone to need me. Is this what neediness looked like, and I just hadn't experienced it? Is this what working at a relationship looked like — and it had been so long since I'd been there I forgot how to recognize it? If I worked at being open-hearted and loving, could I melt her fears? Or had this relationship become like a pair of jeans left too long in the dryer — and would no longer fit?

"I don't think you can ever love me enough," she said.

"I love you. I touch you, I tell you." I stroked her wrist, a weak attempt to reassure her. The moment felt overwrought. I was fatigued from the day in the sun and boosting April's ego. "What do I have to do to love you enough?"

"Be with me more. Spend more time with me."

"I'm with you every spare minute I have," I responded defensively.

"The thing I *like* about you is that you have your own life. The thing I *dislike* about you is that you have your own life."

"What do you want?" I pleaded, desperate for resolution.

"My last girlfriend moved in, gave up her job, helped me in the office, and was with me all the time," April smiled, confidently speaking her truth.

Her wants appalled me. They were the opposite of anything I could offer. "That's not me, or anyone I want to be. That's a housewife in someone's shadow. Is that the only way you can feel loved?"

April was silent. She nodded, "Yes."

"If you are willing to work this through, maybe we've been going too fast and need more time and patience with one another," I said.

"To me working together means being together, a lot," she restated.

"My time to myself, especially for my writing is very precious to me," I explained. "I can't love if I feel I can't breathe, or if compromise feels like dread instead of sharing. For me to open <u>my</u> heart and be happy, I need to feel safe to exhale and be myself. If the price of loving you is every minute of my day, that's more than I can pay."

I stood, dazed. "I need to take some breathing time." I collected the empty glasses, bringing them into the kitchen. Gazing out the glorious dining room window I saw the blazing sun. It looked like a bloody fingertip in the sky, pointing at me to make a move before it got ready to set and wash the beach with darkness. I cleaned the glasses. I rinsed my hands, and then walked towards April. She was still on the deck, watching the sun, looking sad and dejected.

It felt wrong to stay. I realized that I'd never be enough for April. I lived a lifetime with a mother like that, feeling tremendous guilt in not measuring up. Afraid of a romantic relationship with those ingredients, I knew whatever I did, I would only disappoint April. I had to leave, smart enough to see that this wasn't going to work out because of fundamental incompatibility.

"I'm going. It's the best thing for both of us," I blurted, suddenly eager for a hasty exit. I saw her head turn. But I raced out the door before she could catch me.

I jumped in my car, turned up Elvis Costello's *My Aim Is True* as loudly as possible, and prepared myself to brave beach traffic with all the other sunbathers returning to their landlocked lives.

This was the first time *I* ever walked out on a relationship. Usually I was the one who got dumped and rejected by men. They wanted wives too. Yet I entered into liaisons with them knowing of that possibility, hoping the right one wouldn't feel like strangulation. She wanted me to give up my life for her and I still hadn't met her son.

Was my role in relationships with women to be the cold-hearted prick? Have I developed the male energy April said excited her? Where did my newfound confidence come from that let me take charge, choosing to leave an affair that threatened to strangle me? I felt saddened in hurting April, but energized by my ability to do something right for myself.

Would I call April after the weekend and ask for another chance, like I'd done in most relationships before?

Being with a woman brought as much opera as romance with a man, only with less chest hair and curvier waists. My ambivi-sexuality raged on.

19. What Now?
♛ ♛ ♛

After a long, soul-searching drive from Malibu, I threw down my bags and jumped in the shower, hoping the currents of water would wash away my feelings of rage, confusion, and disappointment. The only way I could move on with April would be if I let her control my life. That was a deal killer. What was there about her controlling, clutching behavior that I didn't see? Or did I notice it and just ignore the signs because someone desired me? Speaking of ignoring, I knew I didn't want to deal with my relationship issues just yet. I thought I'd avoid them, like postponing doing laundry, until the last minute when there's nothing left to wear. What was in my future?

Lucky for me, the following Thursday began a three-day writing seminar on "Marketing through Blogging and Social Networking: strategies for marketing yourself on the web, including why and how to create a blog, using social networking effectively for self-promotion, e-newsletters, and more!" I'd get out of the house and yet be able to hide in my work. A great Band-Aid to help heal all of my dilemmas.

Driving to Orange County, I was eager to learn new things. Out of the house and out to make first impressions with real people, so I wore a tasteful black pants suit, light makeup, and sensible shoes. The seminar was at a Hilton Hotel, freeway close. As soon as I arrived, I learned that many events were happening at the hotel that same day. I found the room for my seminar, picked a seat not too close to the lecturer, not too far, with easy access to the exit and the coffee area. I poured a cup, took my seat, and removed a pen and brand new notepad from my giant bag — I read the hand-out that was placed on each desk, eager to learn about:

Why Blog? (Blog vs. Website)

Initial Decisions, such as Branding, Content, and Which Blog Site to Use

Creating a Blog (one lucky attendee will have their blog set up during this seminar)

Promoting Your Blog - Extending Your Reach

Social Networking

I wanted to learn as much as I could. Maybe if I put more focus into my career, my earnings would increase, new opportunities would arise. Anything was possible. The first day's class was taught by a bearded former screenwriter, who was now teaching seminars and doing online coaching for writers. The following day he tag-teamed with a perky recent college grad who spoke in finely tuned Twitter bites.

Her parting words for the day were, "Be brief, but to the point." Go home and search the web. Go to every site you know with new eyes."

That night, under the guise of doing my homework, my fingers found their way to the dating sites I thought I knew too well.

Sure, I knew I wasn't ready to date, but this was class and job-related research. It couldn't hurt to look and see who was out there, so I revisited my *Match.com* account. "As an ambivisexual, should I turn back to men?" I asked myself while heating my Lean Cuisine dinner, just days after my beach blanket disaster.

I remembered what comedian Dana Gould said, *"I keep dating the same person over and over again: Mandy. I loved Mandy. It stands for My, Another Neurotic Disappointment...Yes!"*

Let's try to weed out neurotics. Since single men online seemed so plentiful, I started the search with "Men seeking Women aged 43 to 60." Photos helped. I avoided anyone who looked evil or insane — like Rasputin, Satan, or Dave Navarro.

There were many men, the majority of their descriptions were unmemorable, or as dry and officious as business briefs. They sought a young, spirited, longhaired, affectionate soul, eager to share their lives and ride on the back of their Harleys. Many listed sarcasm as a turn-off. Between my hair, sense of humor, and lack of motorcycle agility, it looked like few from this club would want me as a member.

I remembered what Aldous Huxley said: *I want love, I want poetry, I want danger, I want freedom, I want goodness, I want sin.*

Get out of my mind, Aldous. If you're going to rummage through my head, please do some light dusting and fluff the pillows. Online dating takes a lot of energy, resilience, perseverance, and sanity. I had none of that. I was like a dieter who fantasized about cake. I knew I shouldn't be there. I was recuperating from a break-up and needed time to heal. Internet dating would be waiting for me when I was sane enough for it…and not a moment sooner.

"Lift your fingers and step away from the computer!" I repeated to myself out loud, until I left the room.

Saturday, my last day of class, focused on creating our own websites and blogs. I was eager for that knowledge, hoping I'd now have the tools to stand apart from other freelance self-help writers and zero in on my audience.

The first part of the class was a recap of the last two days. My mind wandered, and I found myself taking many trips to refill my coffee, then leaving the room even between designated breaks to visit the ladies room.

Surprisingly, a wave of sadness and loneliness hit me as I pushed open the ladies room door. Moving to the sink to splash my face with cold water, wishing I could wash away my melancholy, I verged on tears. In this moment I thought I had never felt more alone. Soap in my eyes, I fumbled for towels and bumped into another woman.

"I'm sorry, I couldn't see," I said wiping my eyes, still not seeing.

"Don't worry, take another towel," she said, handing one to me.

I finished drying my face, opened my eyes, and saw her smiling at me.

"I'm Jessica," she said, offering her hand for me to shake.

She was about 45, with long, thick, wavy hair, strong shoulders, a small waist, and dressed for a party.

"I'm Sara, here for a wedding?" I was joking.

"I'm here for my parents' 50th anniversary. They're celebrating half a century. I can't make a relationship last more than a year."

"Me either," I responded.

"Do you ever feel like everyone is happy but you?" she offered.

"All the time."

"Really? Maybe soon will be our time," she added.

"I hope so." I was trying not to stare at her beautiful face. I knew I should reapply my makeup and go back to class, but I was captivated.

"My girlfriend moved out last week," Jessica said, sadly.

"Your roommate?" I inquired, eager to know.

"No. She and I were involved romantically and as soon as she moved in, everything good about us died," she explained. A tear came to her eye.

I got a tissue and wiped her cheek. She smelled of roses and French soap. The nearness of her was a sensual delight.

"Thank you," she said. Her eyes looked into mine and I felt seen and understood. A warm rapport was building. Just then, the bathroom door opened and another woman entered, bringing the outside world into our moment. "I guess I should go back to being a good daughter." She turned away to leave, and then turned back again. "You know, I'd love to continue this conversation. May I call you sometime?"

Surprised, I enthusiastically chimed, "Please do." I reached into my purse, pulled out a card, and gave it to her.

Jessica held the card in one hand and read it. With the other she moved to shake my hand, again. "Thank you, I'll be in touch." She left.

I stayed another minute to comb my hair, reapply my lipstick, and cool down from my quasi-flirtatious encounter, not sure what to make of it. I went back to class feeling a lot more cheerful than when I'd left. The rest of the day in class they showed us templates for websites and blogging. I thought about Jessica, and how odd it was to meet someone like that, and how just like Will, and all the other people who said they'd call, she never would.

Class ended at four o'clock. I got into my car, back to Los Angeles. Traffic was bad; the sun was hot. I chewed gum, played the radio loudly, and wiped sweat from the back of my neck.

I arrived home and eagerly peeled everything off, leaving it in a pile on the bathroom floor. Naked, I scurried to the kitchen for an aspirin and a tall glass of water, to cool me down. As I was gulping and glugging water, I glanced at my phone. The message light wasn't on. Nobody ever called me. I made my way over to the bed, pulled at the blankets, crawled in, and grabbed for the remote control. Another Saturday night alone — just me and my cable channels.

The following day Jessica called. Conversation flowed, as we talked about everything: growing up, our parents, what we were like when we were teen-agers, and if we ever felt cool or geeky. At the end of our two-hour phone conversation, we agreed to meet the next night for coffee and dessert.

She arrived first, looking eager and gleeful. Without makeup she was incredibly beautiful. Jessica saw me and waved. We hugged and shared a self-conscious cheek kiss. After we ordered our tea and brownies, we settled into our cushioned chairs, exhaled, able to relax and take each other in. She wore a sea green halter top and looked girlishly braless. Her tan, muscular arms accented her overall healthiness. Jessica's smile lit up her face, revealing endless cheekbones and wise, understanding eyes.

"Have you recuperated from the anniversary party?" I began.

"Pretty much," she said. "All that happiness and good cheer could put someone in a diabetic coma — unless I could get it to rub off on me, like a lipstick kiss."

I lingered on those last two words, hearing them ever so slowly and wishfully. Our tea arrived. I took a sip immediately. Too hot. Calm down, I told myself and put the cup down.

Ignoring her tea, both eyes on me, she continued. "I'm all for happiness, and celebrating other people's joys. I just wish I had more of my own."

I pinched at the corner of my brownie. "Me too," I said, popping the bite into my mouth. The chocolate was moist and melted easily on my tongue, like a taste of happiness. I quickly had another bite; mouth happy, gazing at Jessica. "Mmm, this is good," meaning more than just the brownie.

She tried a taste now. "This IS good," she answered. "But I try to stay away from sweets. I'm all about balance in my life, moderation, you know."

Jessica acknowledged that she wanted stability and steadiness in her life — instead of insanity. Her outlook was refreshing and sorely needed for me.

I said, "I talk about balance. My goal is to live in moderation. Doesn't always work that way. I want to taste everything. But no heaping portions. Get lots of sleep…"

"Wake up early," she added.

"Are you a morning person? Me too." I took a sip of tea. It was now the right temperature. As I swallowed, it soothed my throat.

"I love the promise of a new day. Anything is possible. See the sunrise, exercise, all good things." Jessica punctuated her statements with graceful hand gestures, as if conducting an orchestra. She sipped her tea genteelly. I noticed her eyes grazing my shoulders and arms. Then the corners of her mouth turned up, as if pleased by the sight. "Do you think you're a passionate person?"

"I have my interests; I guess they're my passions."

"I have my passions," she explained. "I know I need to be touched and receive a lot of affection. Otherwise, I need to get a lot of massages."

I was surprised by her statement. "I get a lot of massages," I lied.

Reaching for my hand, her fingers intertwined with mine, as if eager to begin a dance of intimacy, digits and hands instead of legs and bodies. Her eyes studied me.

"You are a woman who is brimming with passion," she began. "Whoever gets to be with you is quite lucky — especially when you let them unleash your inner zeal."

I breathed deeply, afraid that if I touched her and held her close, I'd never want to let go. She kept stroking my arm, sensuously and intently, as if she wanted me badly and knew exactly what I needed.

"Do you call this balance?" I asked eager to know her intentions.

"I call it a bright beginning."

We spent the evening talking and laughing. I became aware of myself relaxing, and exhaling. I felt safe and accepted. Conversation flowed, like the endless cups of tea we were drinking. We stayed at the restaurant until the waiters put the last chairs up on the tables and mopped the floors. The night ended with a lingering hug goodbye.

The following morning I woke up, got online, and checked my email. There was one from Jessica:

Dear Sara:

I had a very interesting encounter because I was not able to peg you in the first five minutes. You continue to elude me. Most people think I have tremendous gifts and talent and are amazed in my presence. I feel like I am not that special. Now I encounter YOU. You are in a different league — the league I wish I had been playing in all this time, instead of just being the big fish.

I want to LEARN and not get old and stale.

You are the second person in my life to touch me and create this feeling inside that makes me want to devote the next 12,000 hours to just touching you in every way possible that I might give you pleasure. Not as a sexual thing as much as "What can I do to bring you to physical nirvana?" For most encounters in my life, the physical thing becomes just that, there was no spiritual connection. The only other person was a woman in college who, when we met years later, still had that aura about her. It was as if we had never been apart and any physical interaction was cosmic, not animal.

After reading Jessica's email, I exhaled with delight. Is this what I'd been hoping for — someone to bare their soul to me? She's asked me to go deeper — deeper than recent relationships, taking me back to the exhilaration of first dates as a teen — the baggage-free trust of opening yourself to another person. I saw myself diving into a pool of emotional intimacy, rather than just dunking my feet and skipping away like my usual self. She'd unburdened her soul to me, not mere small talk. If I didn't want to fuck this up, I needed to be emotionally present. Wait a minute. How do I know this isn't someone too good to be true who would drown me in their insanity and neediness?

This feels too fast, too good, too soon. It smells wrong. I should be cautious. Jessica is a silky-haired mirage. I labored over what to write back, nothing seemed right.

Luckily, pursuing me, she called the next day. "Sara, I have something to tell you. I hope you don't think I'm crazy."

"Why would I think you are crazy?" I asked, incredulous that we'd be having a conversation that began like this.

"Because I can't see you for a month or two. My aunt Doreen in Michigan just broke her hip. I'm flying today to take care of her. I'd rather go to a museum with you."

"We can do that another time," I said, holding back my disappointment.

"And I can never get decent cell reception at her house. Calls drop off. Let's email in the meantime. Friend me on Facebook. I'll need something to keep me going."

Immediately after hanging up, I signed on to Facebook, searched for, and friended Jessica. I now had 51 friends. Then I noticed correspondence from Derrick:

I'm planning a trip to the Bay Area next week. I was wondering if you were going to be near San Francisco in the next 10 days, so we might hook up. My schedule is somewhat flexible. I eagerly await your response.

Derrick was going to be on the West Coast…eager to see me? A married man with a secure job, wife, and kids…worlds away from my life. He was interested in a fling with a fantasy from his youth? Flattered by the flirtation, this seemed like a bad idea.

I wrote back: Thanks for thinking of me. I live in Los Angeles, a plane ride away from the Bay Area with no plans to be near there. Enjoy your trip.

An hour later Derrick wrote back: *What if I made a stop in L.A.? Would you meet me for dinner?*

One meal with a college flirtation, decades later? That would be harmless, right? I'd write about it. *My Facebook Flirtation.* Maybe *Cosmo* would be interested. They pay well. I wrote back: Don't make a special trip just for me. But if you are in L.A., dinner would be nice. I didn't want to say great — that would sound eager and interested.

That next Saturday I drove to the airport to pick up Derrick. He was a virtual stranger to me. I hardly knew him now and barely knew him 30 years ago. We were in a pottery class together at college, spending Tuesday and Thursday nights together in independent study, sharing studio time — just us, the clay, and the potter's wheel. This was years before the movie *Ghost* where feeling the clay through your fingers and throwing a pot became immortalized as an erotic experience. Then, clay was just messy. Our clothes and hands were always dirty. That's why I primped with extra care today, making sure my hands and nails were perfect. In college his hair was shoulder length, same as mine. Now, in his profile picture there's only a wreath of peach fuzz like a newborn chick that nestles from ear to ear.

I wore my skinniest size-eight jeans to help erase the memory of my big girl size 18 college self. In school, Derrick was so skinny he wore thickly knitted fisherman's sweaters to look like there was some meat on his bones. His slim frame seemed breakable anywhere near my insecure big girl girth. So I never thought of him amorously, and always kept our relationship at arm's length. That's not going to change. Tonight is just dinner, I told myself, then looked in the rearview mirror to check my hair and lips.

Would we recognize each other? I searched my bag for a piece of paper to fashion a sign. I found a printout of an email from Jessica:

Every afternoon having tea with my aunt, I wish I was with you. Hoping to see you soon.

I reread the note, smiled, then wrote Derrick Sanderson on the back in large letters, parked the car, and strode to the gate while straightening my clothes.

The plane from Chicago was on time. People from that flight were walking off the escalator towards baggage. No one looked familiar. I held my sign up and stood so all passengers could see me.

A bald man (with even less hair than the profile photo) in a loosely fitting Italian sweater was at the top of the stairs.

His smile increased as he rushed down the escalator. Was this Derrick? He leapt off the escalator and strode towards me with outstretched arms that he then wrapped around me.

"Sara! You are more beautiful than I could have possibly imagined," he whispered, lips to my ear, in that soothing voice, the one thing that remained unchanged. Surprisingly, this was quite an intoxicating moment. I leaned in and hugged him back. Not sure how long we'd lingered, both breaking from the embrace and back to reality, we took a few steps towards the exit, both eager to be out of there, and in somewhere else.

"Baggage claim?" I said, now walking in that direction.

"No. All I need is my knapsack, right here, same as always. Let's go."

We drove straight to a little Italian restaurant on Lincoln Boulevard, not far from the airport. As soon as we were seated, Derrick studied the wine list.

"Bottle of red to celebrate?"

"Sure," I said, nervous, anxious, and reminding myself that I wasn't on a date. There was a tingling amorous connection here. But I was mindfully aware it was just a nostalgic college dinner with another woman's husband.

"Osso buco for two," he suggested. "Expense account."

"I thought you were a vegetarian?" I offered, remembering.

"That was in the '70s. Now I'm a special occasion carnivore. And this is a very special occasion."

As I was reaching for the bread basket, he reached for my hand. Too startled to recoil, I was curious for him to reveal his agenda. Email communicates only so much.

"I feel as giddy as a school girl," he blushed. "You know I had the biggest crush on you in college. But was too shy and virginal to approach you."

"You were a virgin?"

"I wanted you to remedy that. I was in math club. We were all virgins."

We both sipped wine — to help us swallow Derrick's statement. I was flattered but uncomfortable. A giant salad arrived. He cheerfully and dutifully put salad on a small plate and gave it to me, just like a good dad.

"How are your daughters?"

"I like being a parent. I'm a good dad for daughters. They think I'm sensitive, easy to confide in."

"Yes, that's one of your best qualities. I remember whenever we talked, I never felt like a fat girl."

"I never saw you as fat. You had gorgeous skin and were luscious — with long hair and a warm smile," he said reflectively, like it was last week.

I wanted to make a joke, but thankfully stepped on my own line. As I took a bite of salad, Derrick studied me. "It's good to see that you are even lovelier than I'd remembered. I've thought about you a lot over the years, always wondering what it would be like to be with you."

I stopped chewing. I had a feeling he'd open his heart to me, so why was I taken aback that it was happing? Did I think he'd rather wait till after the main course rather than before? The idiot and the mathematician. Change the subject.

"So you like your job?" I said, trying to cool down the moment.

"I like <u>you</u>, always have," he said, gently turning the heat back on.

"Well, it's nice having dinner with you. I know you are probably tired and have a busy day tomorrow with your conference.

"Slept on the plane. More wine?" he said, beaming, looking at me adoringly.

Here was a kind, loving man, pouring out his feelings — and more wine to me. I should have paid better attention to him in college. If I did, maybe I would have had a good husband, not the crummy one I chose. Good husband. That's an oxymoron for my life. He's someone else's good husband. Don't even think of him like the other men you have dinner with — I reprimanded myself. The main course arrived. I wanted the meal to move quickly now. I thought if I could gently deflect the conversation, I could change the mood and calm his agenda.

Taking a bite, he said, "Everything tonight is great, better than I could have imagined." He looked up to smile at me.

I nodded, but continued eating, thinking that the quicker I ate, the sooner I'd be home in bed, alone.

Derrick talked about cheering the girls on at swim meets, coaching their baseball teams, and hiking with them on Sundays. He was a devoted dad who adored his daughters and never mentioned his wife. So the reporter in me dove in.

"You haven't said a word about your wife."

"Rita? We've become dear friends, confidantes, not so much lovers anymore. I miss that."

"You know, the articles I write help women have better relationships."

"So you have all the answers? You must have great relationships — tell me," his voice lowered.

"No. There's no one. Those who can, are in relationships. Those who can't, talk about them. Those who really can't, write for women's magazines," I joked. Neither of us laughed. In this moment I felt sad for myself, I was face-to-face with a great, stable guy — who was yearning for me — worlds away from the men I knew. But he was untouchable — off limits to me.

After he signed for the check, Derrick touched my hand, and said, "I thought you were a great prize. I was sure someone would sweep you off your feet, love, and cherish you…I always thought about how I'd wished you'd have given me a chance. You never seemed to notice me then. But it's not the '70s anymore. Are you ready to go?"

Back in my car, I drove robotically, searching for his hotel, eager to cool the inner heat and end the evening. As I drove into the circular drive, my heart raced with uncertainty. "Thank you for dinner," I said officiously, as if speaking to one of the blind dates I knew would never have a sequel.

Derrick turned and leaned in. He kissed my cheek and lingered, saying, "I wish you'd come upstairs with me, just for a drink." His voice was soft and inviting like outstretched arms hungering for a heated caress.

I took a deep breath and whispered back, "We both know I should go." I felt pleased that I'd said something mature and kind. Derrick kissed my cheek again and then moved towards my mouth. Another sweet peck, and then he got out of the car.

I watched him walk through the hotel's glass doors before driving away. After turning on the radio, I tried to cool down my overheated self.

As soon as I arrived home, I had to wash my face. While toweling off I thought, this is the closest I've gotten to an emotional connection with a man in two years. It doesn't even feel like anything. So why am I still thinking about him — wondering what his naked chest looks like? Wondering what it would be like to have his hands on me — I closed my eyes and realized my nipples were getting harder. I touched my breasts as my mind raced to what a kiss might feel like. Just as my hand wandered into my panties, Julia called.

"I think you just interrupted a sexual experience," I said.

"You're not sure?"

"It was self-pleasure, following a Facebook date." I remarked.

"Was any of this in the real world, or are you living in cyberspace?"

"Real person. But he's married, from out-of-town, the loathsome double don't. I was going to diddle myself so no one would get hurt."

"Good plan of action."

"Glad you think so. And you?"

I did that earlier today, to break in and celebrate a new vibrator I bought yesterday, after dinner with twin lesbians yesterday. Tonight, cocktails with my neighbor Diego.

"Doesn't he have the mirror on his bedroom ceiling?"

"Yup, it's so disco era. But he's a great cook with a giant cock!"

"Have you given up on love in your life?" I asked, uncertain.

"While love is elusive, I don't want to be sex-starved," Julia said proudly.

"I look up to you…and not with a mirror on the ceiling."

The following morning I called my editor at *Today's Woman* magazine and pitched an article: Facebook *Flirtations, 10 Women Share*. My editor said she'd have to think about it. Then I pitched the idea of a quiz: *Are You Bisexual?*

She said, "Write it up. We'll use it as filler."

20. Are You Bisexual?
☙ ☙ ☙

After drinking a pot of strong coffee, I prepared to compose the quiz. What I loved most about writing self-help articles was getting paid to do my own personal problem solving.

When you're at a party, who do you look at first, men or women?

☐ *men*   ☐ *women*   ☐ *I look for the bar or the food*

How do you feel about touching men's bodies?

☐ *great*   ☐ *fine if they're there*   ☐ *no thank you*

How do you feel about touching women's bodies?

☐ *great*   ☐ *fine if it's there*   ☐ *I don't touch any woman's body but my own*

The phone rang. I turned away from my quiz.

"Sara, I'm going to a party tonight. I thought you and April might want to join me," Beth said, gleefully.

"We just broke up," I said. "I left her after what seemed like an argument that could never be resolved."

"I'm sorry to hear that. I thought she had possibilities."

"Me too. But she's a gorgeous bundle of needy."

"Oh, so you'll be looking for new women," Beth exclaimed. "You seem so happy when you're in touch with your female-on-female self."

"Well, my girl-on-girl side met someone promising," I added. "But I've recently had an Internet encounter with a guy from college."

"You've been busy, hopefully just having a good time."

"The two helped me take my mind off of April. I thought I was starting to fall in love with her, until I felt strangled by her. I recoiled in self-preservation. Does that make me a bad person?"

"No, you're just taking care of yourself," Beth offered. "It makes you a mature and healthy person."

Just then, my call waiting beeped. The other call: April. Oh no, I can't do this, a parachute ride back into crazy town. What does she want? Is she okay? Would she harm herself? I should at least make sure she's safe. I clicked to speak with her.

"I want you to come back. I am lonely without you," April said. It sounded like she'd been crying.

"Please don't cry." I froze. I didn't want to say much, afraid to be sucked in.

"Things can be better," April said in her seductive voice, the one I'd heard that night in the closet. "We can be good together."

"We can be good together?" I just recited what she was saying. This moment felt hollow to me. "We each need time to think about things. Stay strong."

I hung up. I felt her agony though the phone. Knowing I was the cause of her despair brought knots of guilt to my gut. I couldn't even say a joke to evaporate the bad feelings, my usual approach for diffusing tension and pain. So, I just felt guilty. April always appeared rock-hard strong, like nothing could break her. I couldn't change the situation. She needed time. But I knew that soon, once this pain subsided, we'd both find happier, healthier futures.

I clicked back to Beth. "That was her. I've never been on the other end of a woman suffering rejection. I feel horrible."

"I've changed my phone number because of it," Beth said. "Come out with me. There'll be pretty women and men at this party too, creative types, old bohos like us."

"I'm writing a quiz; are you bisexual?"

"Hell, yes. I think you are too. Meet me tonight, you'll get all your Q's and A's," she chuckled. "I'll pick you up at nine o'clock."

Later that afternoon, I checked my email: On Facebook I now had 204 friends. Plus, Jessica felt lonely in the senior community and was still missing me. Derrick had a glorious time and would speak with his boss about more frequent California trips. I turned my computer off, having mixed feelings about my "virtual popularity."

Beth arrived promptly that night, jazzed for new adventures. When we opened the door to the Spanish-style house with a view of the "Hollywood" sign, everyone there looked familiar, yet I'd never met any of them before. Rooms full of attractive, friendly men and women smiled at me. In answer to my own quiz question: *When you're at a party, who do you look at first, men or women,* my answer was — everyone!

Near the food table, Anton, a half-Filipino, half-Chinese writer Beth and I had worked with a few years ago, stopped us.

"Ladies, don't miss the artichoke dip while it's still hot," Anton urged. "Sara, Beth told me you're shopping for a new team...you have a girlfriend?"

"<u>Had</u> a girlfriend," I answered. "We broke up last week."

"Ah. Before I lived with Carlos, I dated women, mainly in college. It was the thing to do, like having a mullet. I love sex with women. But you have to have long conversations with women, listen to their problems, make them feel beautiful. Oy — it takes so much time and energy to make a woman open her legs. Now, a man sees you and says, 'Hey', looks you up and down, and nods as if to say, 'You look fine to me, let's go' and the next thing I know, we're going at it. Nice to see you, Sara. Good luck."

I was surprised by his candor. I grabbed a stick of celery, scooped it into the artichoke dip. Anton was right — at least about the dip. I searched for Beth.

She introduced me to a couple, Jill and Jeffrey, both freelance writer-photographers. They were in the middle of a conversation.

"Why didn't Thompson take your photo book? What happened? I thought he really liked your stuff," Jill asked.

"I wouldn't suck his dick," Jeffrey said.

"You mean you wouldn't schmooze, flatter, fawn, and play the game?"

"No, I mean I wouldn't suck his dick."

I gulped my drink when I heard Jeffrey's comment. There's a lot of sexual energy brewing in this town, right here at this party. I glanced across the room, wanting to get away from the conversation, and noticed a man looking at me. He smiled, nodded, and beckoned me to walk towards the wall he was holding up. He looked smart-ass New York attractive, a smooth-skinned Richard Belzer type.

He kissed my hand, goofy gallant. "I've been watching you make the rounds of this party. I'm Paul. You're quite the mingler."

"Better a mingler than a mangler," I tossed off, with the sarcasm that made average men flee.

"I knew you would be smart," he said, leaning in, as if to tell me a secret. "I noticed you came in with another woman. I know Beth. I've seen her with other women before. If you two are together, I'd love it if you'd take me home with you. My birthday is next week. A threesome would be a great gift."

Disgusted, I pulled away, trying to shake the feeling that I'd been slimed, so I fled to the kitchen. There was a trio of women huddled near the fridge. I politely tried to maneuver past them to the ice chest for a beer.

One woman saw me, broke from the conversation, and said, "Want one of these?" She bent down towards the selection of longnecks in the sea of ice.

"Yes, something imported would be great."

"Try this," she said, yanking one out of the cooler, removing the cap, and then giving it to me. She pulled another one for herself, uncapped it, and clinked bottles with mine. "I'm Theresa. My friends call me TC."

TC was my height, strong-shouldered, with a young face framed by short, salt-and-pepper hair. She could have been any age from 25 to 50. Exuding confidence and sexuality out of every pore, she was a female Rhett Butler, and I was a flighty Scarlett O'Hara.

"I'm Sara," I said flirtily, mind racing for something to talk about. "How do you know our host?"

"We worked on a film together — shared producer credit. I did some camera work, too. I started out as a photojournalist. One picture at a time wasn't enough for me anymore."

"I know what you mean," I said, intrigued by her self-confidence.

TC smiled, walked to another room, parting the chattering cliques as she moved past them, then through the French doors, onto the terrace. I followed her like a scampering pup. She lit up a cigarette and looked me up and down like I was a new car she considered test driving.

"I'm trying to quit. Want one?" she said, enticingly pointing the pack at me. "Some of the people here, it just gets to be too much."

Just then, five loud, tattooed Venice hipsters came out to the terrace. The two men raced to bear-hug TC. The women air-kissed her. She smiled politely, listening to what they had to say for a minute. Then she took my arm and steered me off the terrace, out of the place, and into the street with the speed and agility of a cat burglar. Suddenly we were standing on the silent street in the humid night.

"There's a bar down the street; let's get a drink," she gently commanded.

In the bar she ordered two more beers, *then* checked to see if that was what I wanted. Nodding yes as I looked into her face, I was searching to connect. In that second, she looked away, people-watching around the room. When the drinks appeared, she lovingly caressed her beer and took a big gulp. Finally, she faced me.

"You'd be a good subject for a photo study," TC said. "You've got interesting hands and cheekbones. I'd like to shoot a few rolls with you."

"Really? That sounds great. When would you want to do this?"

TC took another hard swallow of beer. While studying her confident face, I was excited she found me attractive and intriguing — that others sought her out, but she escaped with me. It was a glorious feeling, to be desired by someone in demand, intoxicating, like *Jungle Gardenia* perfume.

"Tuesday. Let's exchange cards and check in, get a plan," she decided. I wasn't sure if I should shake her hand, peck her cheek, or what. Remembering Beth was back at the party, I pocketed her card, excused myself, and left the bar. TC remained behind, poised for another drink.

I found Beth, looking through the host's CD collection. Smiling devilishly, she said, "I saw you leave with TC. What happened?"

"We just went down the street for a drink."

"That's all?" she giggled.

"She said she'd call and schedule a photo shoot with me, thinks I have good hands and cheekbones."

"How seductive. Maybe you'll see her etchings too," Beth said slyly. "I'm proud of your spontaneity. I had my eye on her, but she's clearly interested in you. Go for it. I hear she's a wild woman…never needy."

Thinking back, I compared the man I met at the party — slimy and self-infatuated — with the warm and inviting women — especially TC. How could I fashion this experience into more questions for my *quiz*? Or better yet, how could I find the answers for my own life? My real life, not my virtual life! Felt good to have a choice.

21. Hot Flash
※※※

Later that week, I faced my computer to pitch new self-help articles to my editors about love, happiness, and public acknowledgement of bisexuality. Oops, I thought — that last one was not a story I should pitch as much as one I needed to research, for my own internal editor.

Jessica emailed: *Three days of rain. I feel like I'm in an Ingmar Bergman film, and I'm the only one who isn't speaking Swedish. Wish I could see the sunshine of your smile.*

I paused and thought about her smile, the smell of her hair, and how warm and delicious it felt to hold her close and nestle my nose between her ear and neck. Mmm.

A half hour later, TC called, inviting me to her house in Los Feliz later that day. She told me to bring, among other things, makeup, hair brushes, and a bathing suit. I arrived at her pink stucco 1930s Hollywood bungalow around sunset.

Entering her living room, I saw that all the furniture was pushed to the sides. Aged, woven rugs were scattered around the room, plus prominent dust bunnies in the corners. Professional lights were set up along one wall that had a white paper backdrop spread along its length. There were two cameras with big zoom lenses on the table.

"Hi, come on in," she called, holding a camera, checking the lenses.

I smiled, dropping my weekend bag near the couch. Her manner was as formal as a dental hygienist readying me for my X-rays. It reminded me of my visit to April's office and her polite professionalism. "You brought a bathing suit or halter top? I want to get some shoulder shots and silhouettes."

I went into the bathroom and put on a one-piece halter top bathing suit. Looking in the full-length mirror behind the door, I spied the spider veins on my dimply thighs. Seeing my exposed legs may be too much information too soon, so jeans on over the suit. I slid into a pair of flip-flops, not wanting to encounter the dust bunnies. Exiting the bathroom, I saw TC was sipping from a tall glass filled with clear liquid over ice.

Noticing her beverage, I said, "Can I get some water too?"

"I'm drinking vodka. There's some in the freezer. Help yourself."

The kitchen was a mess — sink full of dishes brimming with grease and food, no doubt untouched for days, if not weeks. I grabbed the sticky door handle of the 1960s egg yolk-colored fridge and pulled gingerly. Blinded by the bright light and lack of food, I saw an ancient tomato, a head of lettuce that had shrunken to the size of a lime, a bowl of lemons, and in the door, three half-full jars of stuffed olives. The freezer was in desperate need of defrosting. Its contents were two half-full bottles of vodka and a pint of white Russian ice cream. I laughed to myself that this looked like a guy's kitchen. Finding a clean glass and some ice, and poured myself a tall vodka. I walked back to the main room, where TC was moving more furniture.

"I'm ready now," she said, fully in charge, looking sexy and in command, wearing black jeans and braless black tank top. "Stand near the window, looking out, but turn your shoulders towards me." TC shot rapid-fire, moving around me like she was a moon and I was the planet. "Tilt your chin up — good. Hand on hip — mmm — turn towards me — good." She stopped, reached for her glass, and gulped. "Powder your face, then come back. We'll try a few shots with the club chair over there, straight from a Joan Crawford press kit. I think you'll like it."

I waltzed to the bathroom mirror and removed the shine from my nose and forehead. Being treated like a fashion model, I felt pretty and desirable. This was the opposite of my date at Ack's house. If this is a date, my companion is admiring me. When I returned, TC was in the kitchen refilling her glass. "More vodka?" she yelled from the other room.

"No thanks, I'm good."

"Yes, you are," she said smiling, walking past me, grazing the length of my arm with an ice chip, which she then slid to her tongue before it melted. She posed me in the chair, gently but firmly touching my shoulders, maneuvering me into a few different positions that simulated glamour shots of 1930s and '40s.

After shooting for an hour, she put the camera down and said, "Ya hungry? Let's order Chinese. Ya like lo mein? Let's get lo mein!"

Before I could even utter a response, she'd speed-dialed the restaurant, barked her order, and hung up the phone.

"They know me. It's like having my own Chinese chef. They'll bring it soon." TC lovingly carried her cameras into another room. She returned instantly, glared at the magazines, old mail, and other clutter on the coffee table. With the sweep of her arm, she shoved the piles of stuff onto the floor next to another heap, no doubt removed the same way. She pulled the coffee table in front of the couch that faced the fireplace. "Ya cold? Want a fire?" TC walked to the side door, grabbed two large logs, swiftly carried them back, knelt down, and lit a fire. As she stood up and brushed off her knees, the doorbell rang. "My magic chef — food's here!"

She opened the door, took the brown bags, and closed the door.

"Can I give you some money?" I offered.

"Nah, don't worry about it. I have an account. I settle up at the end of the month." TC speedily carried the brown bag to the table, then spun on her heel, racing into the kitchen, instantly returning with various plates and utensils.

As she leaned in, I inhaled her delicate scent, freshly showered with a hint of lemon and ginger. Her strong, muscular arms danced gracefully as she orchestrated the table; aged, chipped fine china scavenged from garage sales, mismatched serving spoons, a roll of paper towels, and a coffee can brimming with chopsticks, three-tong forks, and other silverware orphans, clinging close to one another.

"You won't let me lift a finger," I said.

"Please sit," she said. "You are my guest, my lovely model."

I felt catered to and cared for as I sat politely on the couch maneuvering a plate in front of me. TC sat on the floor facing the table. I gracefully slid off the couch to sit on the floor facing her. She dove into the brown bags, ripping them away from the white square cartons inside. Opening the lid of the first carton, she peeked in, then offered it to me, "My dear, please help yourself."

Looking into her eyes before taking the carton from her hand, I was dazzled by her smiling eyes, clearly loving life and guzzling every moment of it, like the tall glass she was still gulping from.

TC opened a clear bag of egg rolls. "Try this," she said, practically shoving the fried roll in my mouth. I took a bite and she smiled. "Good, huh? Not too greasy."

Feeling like I was in the frat house of a college boy, I studied her as I ate. From the waist down, she had the slim legs and flat behind of a boy, with the broad shoulders and large breasts of a commanding matriarch. Her angelic, happy face was girlish and sexy. She was bossy and mannish; testosterone and tits. I guess that's kind of butch. I liked it. I leaned my head back against the couch, sipping the watery vodka, melting into the moment. If there was a romantic interlude tonight, just like the menu, I didn't think I'd be offered a choice. TC would orchestrate it. I'd just wait for the overture.

22. Light My Fire
🔱🔱🔱

The fire was crackling and sparkling, subtly illuminating the room. As TC and I finished dinner, she suggested we move in front of it. She wriggled her legs from under the table, shifting to a place on the carpet a few feet from the fireplace, then patted the spot next to her for me to join her. I eagerly obeyed.

"Beautiful, everything tonight was so beautiful," she mumbled, leaning into me, grazing my clavicle and shoulder with her finger, then nuzzling my neck. "My muse, I think I took some great pictures tonight."

"It was fun posing, being the center of attention" I said, a little dazed by the vodka. Tense and excited by the moment, I thought of other things to say, but I was silent, feeling the heat of her body lean into me, her hard nipples rubbing through her shirt against my bare arm, warm breath on my neck and ear as her mouth snuck up on me with hot, electrifying kisses that melted my anxiety, taking me in, devouring me with her strength, power, and desire. I felt baptized by the heat of her passion. She caressed my breasts, teasing, then squeezing. If a man did this so soon, I'd be angry and turned off. But here it fueled my passion, dissolving my inhibitions.

I groped her breasts, harder than she'd touched mine. TC growled like a lion cub in my ear. Roughly yanking my hair, pulling me down to the floor, she climbed on top of me. I had flashes of thoughts of being with a man. If any guy behaved so animally gruff the instant he touched me for the very first time, I'd be anxious and frightened, or annoyed the way I was with Ack. I'd scoop myself up and leave if I could. But I was easing into this moment, trusting and loving the carnal heat — sizzling, yet safer than being with a man. As TC ground her pelvis into mine, I was electrified. She kissed me hard; I engulfed her mouth ravenously.

TC flipped over so I was on top of her now, both of us writhing in front of the fireplace. Kissing and touching for what seemed like hours, our bodies ablaze with yearning, skin moist with anticipation. I couldn't wait for her to drag me into the bedroom like some prehistoric caveman. Was TC the answer to my Fred Flintstone fantasy?

Suddenly, my senses were frozen by an acrid, burning smell. In my mindless moments of passion, I'd somehow kicked my rubber flip-flops off — and into the fireplace. The noxious odor of burning rubber wafted throughout the house. Our lips parted, awareness came to my brain. I flew off her voluptuous body and jumped to the fireplace in hopes of retrieving my shoes and saving us from a toxic meltdown. I stared into the flames, mesmerized by the color changes of melting plastic oozing over the logs. I felt stupid and careless, like a child who left her toys in the driveway, crushed and run over by a busy parent parking the car.

TC jumped up and retrieved my melted shoes from the fire and tossed them outside, then raced to open all the windows. It was as if a bucket of water had doused our heat as well. "It's been nice, but it's late. We'll catch a movie. I'll call you," she said, ending the interlude, just like Ack.

Tired and dazed by the roller coaster of an evening, I mumbled, "Yeah, good." I threw my bag over my shoulder and walked to the door, barefooted, a disoriented Cinderella. Like a teenage boy with blue balls, hormones raging, I felt I could punch my fist through a glass door and not feel any pain.

Twenty minutes later, I was home. After brushing my teeth, I checked my email. Jessica was missing me. Derrick was reconfiguring his work calendar for more Sara time. I've never had anyone reconfigure for me before. I was flattered by Jessica, but knew she was restless in her situation. I didn't want to get my hopes up that she could ever really be interested in me. Derrick was an online esteem booster. Both were too far away. Meanwhile, in my tactile immediate world, still heady from the ballistic TC experience, I moved to the bedroom to put fresh sheets on the bed. Holding a red pillowcase like a bullfighter's cape, shaking it to tease my imaginary bull, I said to myself out loud, "A relationship on fire — literally. Everything with TC feels larger than life, like opera, a different kind of opera than April's. The bull charges and I step into the ring. Am I a magnet for insane pussy?" I felt heady with confidence, buoyed by my virtual pursuits, so I laughed, like a giggly teen.

"Wash those feet before sleeping on clean sheets," I said, fluffing the last pillow. I bit my tongue, realizing the command was in my mother's voice. Too woozy from the alcohol to tuck the sheets in, I just flopped on the bed and curled up to one of the fresh-smelling pillows — dirty feet and all.

Struggling to keep from feeling dizzy, I wondered, what was I in for now? I was never a bad girl — not in school, not in bed, or anywhere else. TC was brazen and obviously bad. I wanted to taste that fearless, braless freedom. She was someone who made being with her feel like jumping out of a plane — without a parachute. TC was clearly a good-time girl and not interested in a serious relationship. I saw that in neon lights. Did I really want to go down this road? This looked like a good place to hide while I transitioned from April. Maybe this was my mid-life crisis — tasty, like our Chinese dinner.

The next morning it took two strong pots of coffee to kick me into gear to finish my article: *Is He Cheating on You? Ten Ways to Know.* Then I composed a pitch for another piece: *Are You in a Dangerous Relationship?* I sent them to my editor and dashed off to a yoga class. A caffeinated headstand would put my life into perspective.

After yoga, I thought about my world. Friends with kids are moms. Others who are homeowners are unmarried women — it says so on their deeds. I was a non-breeding renter — an old girl. What could I do with that classification? Date young girls so I wouldn't feel so old? Was that the Band-Aid for my ills and anxiety? Isn't that what men do when they have a mid-life crisis? Next I'd be shopping for a sports car.

Life was not a music video, I told myself — not a necklace strung together with pearly passions, four-minute adventures on a sexual high wire. Dig deeper. It was sad to me that I was a self-help writer, churning out advice that got battered women out of trailer parks, encouraged wrinkled soccer moms to moisturize, and yet at the end of the day, I couldn't unravel my own mess.

I learned from Facebook and my now 217 friends that no one ever leaves your life, they just wait for you in virtual reality. Why had Derrick resurfaced? Would Jessica ever return to town? Two safe, long-distance flirtations.

I thought about Jessica, ah, sweet Jessica. I knew she was lonely, so I thought I'd send her an email and some articles about healthy eating and balance — things we talked about when we got together. Also, I went to the *Hallmark* site and sent her a musical card that sang, *Wish you were here.*

I left my apartment to visit the mailbox. Nothing today, not even bills. Junk mail advertisers didn't even want to bother with me! I arrived back to a voicemail from TC, inviting me to the movies, just like she'd promised. I was glad my clumsiness and burning shoes hadn't dampened her interest. I called her the next morning, and we met later that day for the twilight show.

We saw a charming film, *Miss Pettigrew Lives for a Day* at the tiniest theater of the multiplex at *The Grove*. It had maybe 40 seats, smaller than many living rooms. TC had popped her own popcorn and brought it, disguised in a Saks Fifth Avenue shopping bag that also held a thermos of margaritas. She insisted on seats in the last row. I obliged. Only four or five other people in the theater all sat towards the front.

She poured me a drink and opened the popcorn during the coming attractions. We toasted while watching the trailers. Munching on popcorn while the film began, I gloried in feeling like a bad girl, reminding me of the cool chicks who cut classes to smoke cigarettes. TC grazed my cheek with her lips, then moved to my mouth for full-on smooching. My excitement increased as she squeezed my breasts hard through my shirt, reached around, unsnapped my bra, and then speedily raced back to cup my eager, naked breast as the nipple stiffened to her touch.

Just as I was about to gasp, her mouth engulfed mine. I got lost in her fire and urgency. Before I could catch my breath from her killer kiss, TC's hands unzipped my pants. Here? Now? I thought to myself as her hand burrowed into my crotch. She touched me inside my jeans, but over my panties, making me crazy.

I moaned, and she covered my mouth with her lips, muffling the noise, adding to the pleasure. So much for the movie.

TC reached for my hand, directing me to her crotch. I obliged. I glanced up and around the theater — everyone else was absorbed by the film. She skillfully moved her hands, faster, slower, then faster again. Whatever she did to me, I did to her. TC breathed hard in my ear as she whimpered, softly. I did the same. She climaxed first. I came a minute or two later. I wanted to run down the aisle and stand in front of the screen, hands in the air like a prize fighter who'd just been crowned champ. Yay, I am a winner! I whispered to myself.

TC kissed me sweetly now. Then she moved her body away, and went back to her popcorn. She offered me some, as if nothing had happened.

Throughout the rest of the film we consumed the popcorn and margaritas. Blissed and buzzed afterwards, we headed to the bathroom. As I washed my hands. I was listening to two other women who had actually watched the film talk about it. They enjoyed Frances McDormand and Amy Adams romping through London in 1939. I hoped to catch the movie again and actually watch it.

TC washed her hands slowly. As the women left, she said, "Follow me," taking my hand, leading me back into a large stall. I followed, uncertain of what would happen. She clicked the lock behind us. Smiling a devilish grin, she said, "I've been waiting for this." TC grabbed my waist with one hand and unzipped my pants with the other. She yanked my jeans down past my knees, then reached up, grabbing my panties too, pulling them down as she kissed my belly, her tongue making its way down to my hot spot. My breathing accelerated. Her head moved ferociously, fingers grabbing my ass with burning intensity.

My moans were magnified by the reverberations of the tile walls all around us, so excited by the decadence of a private moment in a public space. My titillation fled as I heard the main door open. A small child exclaimed, "Mommy, I have to pee *now!*"

TC and I broke our moment of passion with laughter. I was now drowning in a full body hug, as she leaned against me, pressing me into the stall wall. I felt one with her and part of the wall. We were both moist with passion, excitement, and the heat of the confining space.

I kissed her ear lobe, then licked the saltiness along her neck, reminiscent of the popcorn we'd devoured a few orgasms ago. This was opera! I laughed to myself, remembering my late date with the tenor. If Diana could see me now!

As soon as the restroom was silent, we unlocked the stall and slinked out of the bathroom. While riding the down escalators to the parking garage, we gazed at each other, smiling. TC licked her lips. I blushed. We shared a quick, friendly hug before getting into our cars.

At home I checked my email: Four new Facebook friends. Jessica was returning home. Derrick was coming back to town too. And he'd changed his relationship status on Facebook to: *It's complicated.* One of my editors emailed me too. I learned my pitch was accepted: *Are You in a Dangerous Relationship?* I now felt really well-equipped to write it. Did I need a score card for my own life?

23. Are You In a Dangerous Relationship?
※ ※ ※

No hello. TC just blurted, "Sara, those pictures I took of you. They're great. Can't wait to show you the prints. Meet me later today. C'mon, I'll pick you up."

Feeling hesitant — did I have the energy to be with TC? I was an old girl without life insurance — "Well…"

"Come on, babe, you look so beautiful. I printed some of them in sepia, and you look like a goddess. I can't wait to worship you," she crooned.

"Okay," I said, caving to worship.

At 5:30, TC's dusty Corolla was at my door, windows and sunroof down. She was in a tank top and shorts, beaming, looking like a teenager. I got into the car, and she gave me a sloppy kiss. "Hey, babe." She reached down, taking a swig from a nearly empty bottle of Jack Daniels. "Want some?" Her voice sounded a bit slurred.

"Should you have that in the car if you're driving?" I asked, concerned.

"If you hold the bottle, I can drive," she cooed, impishly.

"Maybe I should drive," I offered.

"Nope, I'm in charge. Baby, you can't drive my car," she sang, giggling.

"Should we stop and get coffee?"

"No stopping, no coffee…no ruining my buzz!" she slurred again, almost missing a red light.

"Stop!" I gasped.

"Are you criticizing me?" she said angrily.

I shook my head "No," eyes on the road.

"Last time we were together you were a lot more fun," she said.

"That's because you weren't drunk," I snapped.

Come to think of it, I'd never seen her sober. "We met two months ago and you think you know all about me, is that it?" she fired at me.

"We met two weeks ago," I said, sternly.

"Correcting me like the dreaded nuns from Catholic school," she mumbled. "That could be debated too."

"I don't want to debate. Where are we going?" I was concerned.

"I'm taking you to the studio to see your pictures. Just through the canyon. Keep your shirt on — or let me be the one to take it off." She grabbed my left breast. I twisted away from her. TC stopped at a red light. There was a car in front of her. When the light turned green, he didn't move. She jumped up, poking her head through the sun roof yelling, "Go, fucker, go."

He sped off and she followed, on his tail. Both took the road's many turns too fast. The empty bottle rattled on the floor near my feet as the car swerved. His car disappeared onto a side road. TC sped up, pleased with herself. The wind whooshed through the windows as she raced down the leafy road.

TC turned to me, slurring, "Come kiss me, babe. Come closer, kiss me."

One minute the car was speeding along, then TC suddenly swerved. Next we were careening through the air like superheroes in the *Batmobile*. Or was it Dorothy from *The Wizard of Oz*? I grabbed for the dash as we thudded down, and the front of the car bolted into a thick tree by a grassy ditch, accordioning into the tree. The engine was smoking. The breeze drifted in through the sunroof.

My head jerked back with the jolt; knees banged against the glove compartment. I saw shards of glass along my arm. What a pretty design it made. Then I realized I was cut and bleeding in many places and felt stinging where glass gashed my arm. I was dazed but miraculously alive. TC was slumped over the steering wheel. I shook her. She opened her eyes, mumbling, "What happened?"

Other cars stopped. People opened our doors to see if we were all right. Their voices sounded like static. I got out, stood up, making sure my arms and legs could move without pain. My right arm hurt. I circled it a few times as the pain subsided. Rivulets of blood slithered down to puddle at my wrist.

I gazed back into the car. TC was breathing and talking to herself. Good, she was still alive. I was relieved. She looked so wrong and uninteresting. I now knew that I wanted to be far away from her once this mess was over. Before the police came, I reached in, grabbed the bottle of Jack and hurled it into the ditch. I couldn't let it be obvious that she was drunk in the car. When the police arrived I tried to do the talking, but I was disoriented, not making sense. Everyone looked fuzzy and was speaking slowly. An ambulance arrived. They examined us, and miraculously, we just had cuts that were cleaned and bandaged. We were taxied home, separately. I was angry with both of us for being so sloppy and out of control. How could I be in that moving car with an angry, amorous drunk? My feelings weren't love for her, or for myself. What a rocky road of self-destruction. I hoped this derailment would be a wake-up call for me.

On the ride home I thought about TC and how she controlled the relationship 100%. She was bossy and manly, not soft and cozy — or someone to cuddle and spoon. We'd never even been in a bed together. TC made me feel like I could stand naked on the roof of a moving car and sing — and she'd be egging me on. But that wasn't someone to grow old with. I'd die trying.

I called TC at home the following day. She never returned my call. We'd crashed on the road James Dean had died on. But he was in a hedonist's sports car, not an old Toyota with a high safety rating. People die in accidents like this. I couldn't let death win. With less than a half century left, I didn't need to add the exhilaration of a near-death experience to my list of sexual exploits. I walked away from the relationship to save my life. I hoped TC would save hers.

Would I let this event change me for the better? Or would I continue to jump at self-destructive thrills? This wasn't a mid-life crisis or bad-girl behavior — it was simple stupidity. I should be my own mother and ground myself! Lock me in the house for a time out to figure out my life — not just my next fling. This crazy teen-age behavior and sexual flip-flopping would make me a pretty corpse too soon. What now? How could I let death get this close?

The following day, my horoscope read:

You are currently stuck between two strong desires: The desire to create for your own pleasure, and the desire to please and seduce others. You come by this latter urge naturally, as it is part of your character. It will understandably be difficult for you to resolve this dissonance. The solution, for you, is in asking yourself why you feel such a strong need to be appreciated.

I reread my horoscope three times and realized that sometimes when I was really hungry for a meal, I'd been known to gorge on French fries. Same with relationships. I was so tired of being alone, that I'd rather gorge on the thrill of sex and the hope that it could worm its way up from a genital euphoria through my body into a loving, caring, heartfelt place. It had all been such a bad, disastrous idea. Fifty, behaving like 15, won't get me to 51! Hadn't I learned anything from my birthday intervention? Had I reached the rocky bottom of a dateaholics crash too? But how should I balance my disaster factor with my inner chasm of aloneness? No ice cream, cheesecake, or chocolate kisses either! Mmm, chocolate kisses — the only kisses I might be having for a while.

24. Stick Shift
🐚🐚🐚

After too many dating disasters and a near-death experience, a loving relationship seemed worlds away. My birthday intervention set that goal so far out of my reach that I knew I felt too shattered and ill-equipped to seek it out. "Just enjoy yourself," was supposed to be my mantra. But I still hungered for love to breathe life into my stone-hearted, fragile self-esteem. I needed to launch a new plan: Why not go in another direction, using wisdom and healthy sensibilities? I knew the lessons of self-help advice by heart: The most important loving relationship was the one with yourself, not someone else. How about figuring out how I could like myself, and love myself too?

I called my touchstone, Julia. She'd been out of town, visiting her mom. It was so long since we'd spoken, I never even told her I was seeing TC.

"You're not going to believe what I'm doing now or what I've been doing since we last talked," I began. "I just stopped seeing a woman who almost killed me."

"Do tell." Julia was intrigued.

"I was seeing this woman, TC."

"Teresa Catherine? You met her?" Julia was incredulous.

"Met her, we've been lovers the last two weeks, until she almost killed us both," I said. "You know her?"

"Sounds like her and her excitement factor. I had a crush on her. She gallivants at Outfest every year. Her promiscuity is legendary. Some gals thought TC stood for tough cunt. Sorry it got so dangerous."

"That hottie from hell has driven me back to reevaluating my dating strategies."

"Again?" Julia remarked, sighing.

"That painful probe of an intervention you seduced me into sitting through helped me see I should *hunt* like a man, and just have a good time. I'm giving myself a month to meet a guy to have a few dates with, see if something can develop; if not, I'll go back to women feeling confident, no more ambivi-sexual.

"Wow, strong words. Should I believe you?" Julia asked. "The point of that event was to get you to relax and crank back the hunt. Chill about it all, rather than burn to meet and greet."

"I'm not looking for a life mate; I'm looking for a weekend, or a month of hook-ups and connection. Enjoyment. That's the birthday mantra, right?" I asked, hoping my plan was not absurd, while trying to win Julia over.

"Take a breath, take two breaths, and at least a week off! Get still and stop searching. Don't you see how obsessive you are? Sit with your emotions and feel your feelings."

"I don't like my feelings. I don't want to be alone with them!" I said, churning in my own sadness.

I heard Julia sigh; I knew it was difficult for her to hear me speak my pain. "Listen, you have so much in your life," she began. "I wish you could focus on everything else other than d-a-t-i-n-g. Put it out of your mind, for a while. You know, it's overrated and only brings more angst than pleasure. Besides, you'd give up men and retire your penis tree-climbing gear? You've been on the hunt for men, their approval, and male sexuality your whole life. Would you know how to stop?"

"Yup, if it doesn't work out this month," I said, half-certain.

"I don't approve. But if you must, remember, this month has 31 days in it, not 30. Are you giving yourself the extra day?" she said, giggling.

"Yeah, I think I'll need it," I responded. "I want to stop. I don't necessarily know how to. I've been programmed since birth to seek daddy's approval and society's. Not that either have noticed me or mattered for years."

"Don't trash your man-hunting gear so soon. I know you…just stash it in the back of your closet."

"You mean the one I'll have to come out of eventually?"

"Touché. The one I'm in — denial."

"At least we'll be together. I like that." I answered.

"You don't really have to pick a team. I'm not, and I'm not worried about it," Julia said. "Just take it slow…you'll find your happiness."

I knew she was right, but I was still uncertain. "What does happiness look like and how will I know when I've found it?"

"Haven't you written self-help articles about this? Just experience someone's company and stop asking yourself questions. Try that. See yourself in the ocean being calmed by the water instead of you trying to be a wave. How's that for a start?"

"Good beginning, I'll try it." I said. So I thought I'd heed her words and start with a relaxing bubble bath. I cleaned the tub and found my best bath salts, turned on the water, and took off my clothes. Just as I was getting into the tub, the phone rang.

"Sara, it's Jessica! I'm back in town. Want to go to the museum on Saturday?"

"Sounds great," I said.

"Botticelli would be more beautiful viewing it with you," Jessica whispered.

I walked past a mirror on the way back into the bathroom, catching a quick glance at my unclothed form. Not bad, I thought to myself, Botticelli would approve.

We met on Saturday, at the top of the steps of the L.A. County Museum. Wind swirled around her, fanning her wavy copper hair, so she, too, resembled a Renaissance beauty, a Rembrandt muse. We hugged hello. Jessica's freshly washed hair surrounded my face, smelling like maple syrup and mint tea. The embrace lingered, neither of us wanting to be the first to let go.

We walked through the museum, exploring centuries of beauty, discussing brush strokes, lighting, and composition. I was looking at a painting and gazing out of the corner of my eye at Jessica. A few seconds later, I saw her turn to study me. We hugged again. After almost two hours of art exploration and surreptitious admiration, we stopped for coffee at the museum cafeteria.

"With you, these paintings look all the more beautiful to me," Jessica said.

"Your eye for color and composition is amazing."

"Years of graphic design, drafting, and architecture kick in all the time," she added. "When design jobs slowed down, I got my real estate license. The designer's eye helps me with staging houses so they sell faster. I see things most people overlook. You should see me dress up a short sale."

"I believe that," I said, admiring her diversity.

"When I look at you, I see a bright, intriguing woman searching for a companion and a soft place to land," she said taking my hand.

I marveled at her perceptiveness. We stood, tossed our coffee cups in the trash, left the cafeteria arm-in-arm, walked down the stairs to the side of the museum, the sculpture garden, where all the Rodins lived. Gazing up at them, we glanced back at one another for a loving embrace.

The hug melted into a heated, caring kiss that was passionate, yet safe and sane. I felt cherished. Things between us were fresh, new, and exciting, yet not about larger-than-life adventures, desire on fire, or taking bigger risks than before. With each caress, I felt my heart opening. This moment wasn't filled with opera or insanity. It felt like rebirth — life itself. I felt happy, peaceful, and for the first time in a long time, safe to be myself. I'd learned from my past not to hold too tightly to the future. But I felt happy and hopeful because neither of us wanted this moment to end. Safe and sane — that was my new mantra. I repeated it to myself over and over, all the way back to my place.

I went home to an emergency call from my editor. Could I write up *5 Ways to Get Close... Fast* and turn it in by midday tomorrow? After my day today, it was easy.

5 Ways to Get Close... Fast

Like yourself. Approach each date with confidence. You are worthy of being treated well and entitled to have a good time. If you can convey those feelings to your new man, he'll have a good time too.

Relax. He's nervous too. Sometimes sharing your feelings, or even saying, "Ya know, I'm kind of nervous tonight," may put both of you at ease.

Find points of common interest. Hobbies, friends, movies, a love of animals...Have one or more of those in common and you've got the basis for a strong conversation that could lead to a strong relationship.

Regard him as a person and not a marriage prospect. Men sense when a woman has marriage on her mind. It makes them excuse themselves mid-dinner and never want to return.

Treat him the way you would want to be treated. Compliment his new tie. Thank him for showing you a good time. Let him know you'd like to see him again. If the chemistry is right, you will.

I could write just the right answers effortlessly. Living them, that was my challenge. I reread my piece again, hoping my advice would sink in…into me!

I now had 250 Facebook friends, plus daily emails from Jessica and Derrick. Her I was thrilled with…Derrick not so much. What did his new status, *It's Complicated* mean? We didn't even kiss deeply. I hope he's not thinking of leaving his wife for me. Whenever I thought of him I was filled with discomfort and excitement, reminding me of the dominatrixes I saw, and the men in diapers, the spank followed by the gentle caress schizophrenic and scary.

25. School Daze?
♛♛♛

Derrick's latest email: *I have another business trip on Friday. I'm making it a weekend. So I can see you — dinner Friday night?*

His boyish eagerness made me feel desirable — instead of my usual — invisible, so I said yes. Dinner was at a romantic restaurant with candlelight and wine. Derrick spoke slowly, softly, and sweetly about our last dinner together.

"And then you changed your Facebook status. Why?" I quizzed him intently.

"Being out of Chicago reminded me of the world I've been hiding from. The routines of family life don't give me time for reflection or for myself," he explained.

"What's changed?"

"Me!" he said, smiling gleefully. He raised his wine glass to his lips, sipped, and then gazed deep into my eyes as if downloading his thoughts with one blink. "I'm more than a dad with teenage daughters. I didn't feel it in the core of my being — the way I do now. Besides, my wife has her interests and friends — that don't include me. So I should have my own life, too. We don't share a bedroom anymore. I'm living in my home office. That way the girls keep their continuity."

"It sounds disruptive," I murmured.

"I've never been happier," Derrick insisted.

Neither of us wanted dessert or coffee. After we walked out of the restaurant, he leaned in for a hug. I complied. Back at his hotel as my car turned into the main entrance, Derrick touched my hand, commanding, "Park. Come up with me."

I did as I was told. We walked into the hotel together, into the elevator, each not saying a word. When we got to his floor, Derrick took my hand and held it until he put a key in the door. He turned on the light, took my things, then lunged into me for a passionate kiss and body-to-body caress.

His ardor was contagious. Both hungry for affection, here was our buffet for feasting. Clothes unzipped, unbuttoned, and dropped to the floor with lightning speed as we stepped closer to the bed. Derrick, his taut but not Ack-like buff torso had a few fine clumps of light brown hair. He pulled the top bedspread back and politely ushered me to lie down on the crisp white sheets. This was not a soccer dad tucking his girls in for the night.

Derrick and I seemed magnetized together, with a Velcro-like compulsion, needing as much skin as possible to touch the other's nakedness, while kissing and devouring one another, as if the sex-starved hunger would never end. Why was I so hungry? After so much time thinking about Jessica, how could I be here, now? I told myself it had to do with fulfilling college fantasies and resolving my urges for men.

After what seemed like hours of kissing and caressing, Derrick took charge and penetrated me, his athletic torso and muscular arms proud, graceful, and confident. His eyes open, studying me, pleased and delighted to be where he was — not closed and hiding in fantasy like others who wished they were with someone else while inside me.

I could tell that Derrick was ready to come — sooner than he wanted to. So he now closed his eyes and did some energetic breathing to hold on a little longer. But ultimately he collapsed exhausted, still wanting to hold me.

Me on the other hand, I saw this as a one-time thing. Something I'd thought about that I finally got to do — like meet a Beatle or visit Morocco. I lay still, waiting for Derrick to move or say something.

After about two minutes he kissed my neck and whispered, "You're sweeter than I imagined." Then for the first time since we'd entered the room, he rolled away from me to the other side of the bed, flat on his back, gazing up at the ceiling. "I've thought about this moment for 30 years," he said, reflective and satisfied.

That statement made me uncomfortable. I sat up on the side of the bed, ready to dress and go home. Derrick's hand traced my back, then soothingly stroked my spine.

"Stay with me. Neither of us has anywhere to be in the next few hours. I want to hold you." Derrick rolled towards me and put both hands on my shoulders.

Overwhelmed by his want and desire, I stayed, telling myself, "Leave at sunrise and be done. That way no one can get hurt."

Morning broke, and I awoke wrapped in Derrick's arms. "Is this what it feels like to combine sex and love together?" I said to myself, delighting in the wondrously cozy feeling. I knew I had to leave, if for no other reason than to avoid morning awkwardness. I slithered out of his caress and into my clothes. I exited the room silently, certain that getting back to my apartment would help me reassemble clarity.

Back home, I stripped off my clothes and jumped in the shower, eager to wash away last night. Was this feeling the male energy April liked about me? Or was I taught well about cowards' behavior from the men who slithered away from *me*?

As I toweled off, I heard the phone ringing. Oh no, it's Derrick, I thought. I clicked the caller ID: Jessica. "Hello!" I chirped, gleefully yet guiltily.

"Sara, it's Jessica. I'll be in your neighborhood in a little while. I was wondering if I could stop by for tea? I'll bring fresh croissants!"

Freshly showered and tingling with popularity, I cooed, "Sure, what time?"

"Will 11 work for you? I hope you don't have lunch plans."

"11 is fine. I'm still full from dinner," I said, smiling to myself, knowing full well I was talking about the course after the main meal. The minute we both hung up I hurricaned through my apartment, cleaning, hiding clutter, the fire drill of rearranging so it looked like a home and not a cage.

Jessica arrived on time, all smiles, smelling as delicious as the pastries she brought. After breakfast I showed her around the apartment. When we got to the bedroom, she took my hand and pulled me to the bed, proceeding to make out with me. Long, passionate kisses, reminiscent of just hours ago — I felt like the prom queen of my own passion-a-thon weekend. Confident and buoyed by all the attention, I undressed her. She raced to unhook my bra. As she nibbled my nipples, the scent of her hair and skin was intoxicating. We raced to be naked and explore each other's bodies. I felt graceful and young, new and hopeful — only positive feelings. I've never known myself to be this optimistic. I was exhilarated by passion, fueled by affection, nurtured by the attention. Was this still safe and sane behavior? Was it the weekend or was it Jessica? I dove into her with every life-affirming breath of my vibrantly beating heart.

Kissing Jessica tasted like sanity. Each embrace and loving stroke felt as though it was coming from a caring place. Her skin was a whipped cream dream, unflawed by scars or bruises. She was sweet and kind, and affectionate on a bed, unlike TC who said beds are places for folding laundry and hiding bills underneath.

"Slow down your brain," I told myself, realizing I'd only spent mere hours with her, but feeling heady with hope like after my first school dance. As soon as we were spent, I got up and brought back chilled glasses of water to revive our parched selves.

"You're a delight," she said. "I've thought about you all these weeks away. Now my imagination gets to be in the real world…on real skin," she said, while tracing my arm with her finger, then following the line with her lips.

The phone rang. I dreaded who it might be. So, I didn't answer it. I just wrapped my arms around Jessica and closed my eyes.

26. Mouseburger No More!
♛ ♛ ♛

When I began selling stories in the self-help world, the moment I felt I was really good at it was when I sold my first piece to *Cosmopolitan Magazine*, or *Cosmo*. The doyen of women helping women in the self-help world was then editor-in-chief Helen Gurley Brown. I admired her career. She coined the phrase "Mouseburger", defining her readers as women who are "not prepossessing, not pretty, don't have a particularly high IQ, a decent education, good family background, or other noticeable assets." If they apply themselves seriously according to her rules, Miss Brown said, such women could have "deep love, true friends, money, fame, satisfying days and nights." All you need to compensate for your modest endowments is "street smarts," good intuition, a degree of selfishness and drive. She did it with these qualities, she argues, and her "mouseburger" readers could too.

Some days in my past, I resembled the mouseburger persona. But not today, no way! Overnight I went from lonely and alone to adored and devoured, by more than one person, more than one team. I'm saying this mainly for myself, because I'm so stunned and amazed by my newfound appeal. I don't think I've changed significantly to warrant such attention. Maybe the lottery of loneliness just picked my ticket to have a new kind of life. Whatever the reason, I'm ready for more.

At a time in life where I thought I'd be overlooked or unloved right through to my years in an assisted living facility, my newfound popularity, desirability, and ambisexuality has rocketed my self-esteem to the moon and beyond.

As soon as Jessica kissed me goodbye, I raced to my computer, eager to fire off story pitches about finding love and desirability:

15 ways to be more desirable

8 tips to keep him coming back

Facebook *flirtations: love at your fingertips*

Date till you drop: the do's and don'ts of seeing more than one person

12 lies that lovers tell, and how not to get caught in them

I guess any of my editors could see what was going on in my mind and in my life. Meanwhile, Derrick called later that day, Saturday afternoon. I told him I was working. He asked if we could have an early dinner as he had a 7 a.m. flight tomorrow. This felt safe and sane to me. Or as I said to myself, "Sometimes dinner is just dinner. A girl has to eat."

When I got to his hotel room, it turned out he'd planned dinner with room service. The silver trays had already arrived with a chilled bottle of champagne. A warm bubble bath was running. Two robes were being heated on the towel warmer in the luxurious bathroom.

I'd originally envisioned the evening as something public and speedy. Charmed by his efforts, I found this all terribly romantic. But I knew dinner with bubbly and bubbles with a man who was catching a plane in 12 hours was fleeting. I believed this whole adventure was his orchestrated fantasy, and I was the living, breathing prop of his castle in the sky. It felt yummy and hedonistic for me to play along. I felt important, respected, and appreciated. After a warm hello that included an engulfing hug, passionate smooching, and bra unhooking, I undressed to slide into the tub, while Derrick popped the champagne cork. *Creating a Romantic Night:* This would be a good story to write about, I thought to myself, as he handed me a chilled champagne flute.

Then Derrick slipped into the relaxing warm water. His assertiveness turned to shyness as the water soothed our anxieties and the realization of who, what, and where sank in. He spoke softly and gently, "My time with you has changed my life."

"Me too," I added, feeling champagne bubbles teasing my tongue while trying to fashion the soap bubbles to camouflage the fleshier parts of my arms and thighs.

Derrick was now amorous and passionate, nibbling on my ears and neck. "You make me feel alive and manly," he whispered. While pouring more champagne he said, "This weekend has filled me with amazing memories."

"Me too," I whispered in return. But I was starting to feel anxious about spending so much time together, concerned he might be overreacting or clingy. "You need a good night's sleep to catch an early flight."

"This weekend would be perfect if I could sleep and dream with you in my arms before flying back to my life."

How could I say no, gotta go, to a request like that? We toweled off and got into bed. We were both very tired, and fell asleep.

Around 4:30 a.m. I heard Derrick rustling around, packing. I grabbed my stuff and went into the bathroom. After washing my face, I put my underwear back on.

As I dressed, I realized my phone, sitting on the bathroom sink, was vibrating. Jessica had left me a message, "Where are you? I have a breakfast surprise for you. Call me, so I can tell you where to meet me at 10 a.m. tomorrow."

I texted back, "Researching a story, call you at nine a.m. tomorrow." The second I turned off my phone, a surge of guilt raced through me. Derrick was more life experience and article fodder than someone I could be serious about, right? Was I going to spend the day with Jessica after a night with Derrick and four hours sleep?

I'll sleep on Monday.

I dropped Derrick off for his plane promptly at six a.m. He gave me a peck on the cheek and whispered, "I have so much to thank you for."

"Me too. Safe trip." I drove away feeling exhilarated and tired with every breath. I thought it was my heightened self-esteem that made being with Jessica so effortless. As I drove through Los Angeles Sunday morning, before the sun was up, while the city was still asleep, I was one of few cars on La Cienega Boulevard. Watching as the sun crept through the clouds to commence the morning, bliss surged through me. I experienced a new sensation, a sense of not feeling alone.

Back home by 6:45 I debated about sleeping till eight a.m. I set two alarms and jumped into bed. After what seemed like 10 minutes later, the alarms roused me from deep sleep. I dressed, ready to meet Jessica, dialing her number at exactly nine a.m.

"Good morning, my pretty," she answered the phone. "Can you meet me at 10 this morning? I have an open house today and need to set up ahead of time. It would be great if you could meet me there, help out, and I'd show you around…sort of a rehearsal for prospective buyers."

"Sure," I said, still feeling shell-shocked and monosyllabic. I wrote down the address and met Jessica at a cozy cottage in Laurel Canyon. When I arrived, the front door was open. Jessica was in the kitchen, dressed in a suit, putting mounds of cookie dough on a baking tray.

"Glad you're here," she said smiling. After kissing my cheek, she grabbed a finger full of raw cookie dough and held it to my lips, "Want some?" she offered.

"Always," I answered, opening my mouth, so I could taste the sweetness.

"We bake cookies, so the fresh-baked smell wafts through the house, creating a scent of hominess." She wiped her hands on a dish towel, then gently grabbed my arm. "Let me show you around," she said, modulated, rehearsing her professional spiel. "On our right we have the dining room with a picture window and view of the garden…cherry blossoms, a shady tree, great for outdoor entertaining. Up these stairs which have the original 1940s carved banisters, you'll find three bedrooms which are also suitable to be home offices or media rooms."

"Lovely patter, I'd buy what you're selling," I offered, as she took my hand and walked me from one room to another, pointing out the Anderson windows, skylights, and other amenities.

Just as we were leaving the master bedroom, which had a fireplace and floral patterns on the bedspread and drapes, she turned to me and said, "I'd love to sell ya something." Jessica reached for me, circled my waist with her arm, and kissed my mouth, passionately. The next thing I knew, I was on the bed and she was taking my pants off.

"Aren't you supposed to be working?" I asked, titillated by the moment.

"I'm working on you…it takes the edge off of open house jitters."

I reached for her and removed her jacket, then unzipped her pants, slipping my hand into her panties. She was warm and wet. I was thrilled to be in the moment, and with her. We groped, kissed and bit each other's bare behinds. I tasted her sweetness. As soon as she moaned, I heard a man's voice.

"Hello? Is anyone here?" said a male voice emanating from the kitchen.

"Up here," Jessica yelled down as she bolted up, collected her suit, and frantically searched for her panties. "Just some last-minute details. I'll be right down. I'll meet you in the kitchen."

"Panties? Here you go," I said softly, offering them to her.

"You need to go. I'm sorry, I thought we had more time. House buyers can be eager beavers."

"Real estate brokers have sexy beavers," I said, licking my lips.

"Get dressed and slip out the back door," she requested, business-mannered, while putting on her left shoe and straightening her collar. Jessica kissed my lips then popped some Tic Tacs into her mouth and raced downstairs.

I finished dressing, moved to the mirror, and smiled at myself with an air of fearless self-satisfaction. "Nobody could call me a mouseburger now," I said while brushing my hair. "I like being 50." My mature self looked me in the eye. Was being with Jessica still a sane experience — practically getting caught in someone's bed? In my defense, I thought — we were actually in a bed and not a moving car — spontaneous with time constraints. Future events would reveal the sanity quotient.

On my way home I stopped off for some groceries. At the checkout line I impulsively tossed a bag of Ruffles cheddar potato chips into my basket. I chomped on chips the entire ride home, replaying the weekend's highlights in my head and smiling.

Back in my apartment, I took off my clothes and threw on sweat pants and a tank top. Checking my email, I saw Derrick thanked me for the weekend. Jessica wrote too, stating, *"You're my lucky charm. Within one hour we had two offers on the house. I'm bringing you to "help" me with all open houses."*

On Facebook I now had 268 friends. I'd never felt this popular or in demand in my entire life. In spite of reconnecting with Derrick, I was still skeptical about Facebook. What constituted a "friend"? Was it someone you met at an event and could now contact freely for future meetings and networking opportunities? Sure, someone will "friend" you on the Internet, but will they meet you face-to-face? Or pick you up from the airport? In L.A. airport-driving friends are highly regarded. You always return their phone calls and send holiday cards every year. Thanks to Facebook, I had a whole new world of people to keep up with, and who'd keep up with me. Most would never even meet me for a cup of coffee.

27. Real Love? Real Estate
♛ ♛

Fueled by my rockin' intimate life, I embraced my role as Yoda of love and sexpert diva with new vigor. Worlds away from thinking I had all of the answers, I knew I was on to something exciting and esteem-building. I just had to digest it all — and rest up from my weekend.

Writing flowed through me. I dashed off a snappy sidebar: *What Your Taste in Men Reveals About You.* My types were:

The Eternal Child

The Silent Type

The Rebel

"Ugly" Men

Macho Man

Men Who Won't Commit

Men Who Commit Too Soon

Just Like Your Father

The Winer Diner Chaser

Man Under Construction

Mr. Mirror

Mr. Stable

After finishing that article, I rewarded myself by watching a movie, with a snack. My choice was *Sleepless in Seattle* with a pint of Haagen Dazs, honey vanilla. You'd think I'd back off from ice cream, comfort food of rejection, especially since it packed on belly fat at a time when my nakedness was front and center. But old habits die hard, and still live in my freezer. I followed the film with a bubble bath. As much as I liked being in high demand over the weekend, I still liked being in my fortress of solitude, in the bottle city of Kandor.

Around sunset, I checked my email. I now had 266 friends on Facebook. That was two less than before. Dos amigos had unfriended me. Who were they? I searched through the thumbnail smiles of my "friends." I wasn't exactly sure who left my page. But I was glad it wasn't Derrick or Jessica. I ended the day watching the last half of *Casablanca,* identifying with Ingrid Bergman's Ilsa, having feelings for Rick and Victor. She had a choice between romance and excitement, or sanity and consistency. She chose the latter but pined for the former. Is it wrong to be seeing two people at once? I've never really been in that situation before. It's not like Derrick lives here. He'll get tired of me soon, and the scenario will fizzle out. I fell asleep as the end credits rolled.

Morning: rolled out of bed, made coffee, checked email. Derrick will be spending this next weekend with his daughters attending their swim meets. I was relieved. But he thinks his feelings for me are growing warmer than the bubble bath we shared. That's not good. I hope spending more time with his daughters will help him see that they are his true priority. An editor at *Marie Claire* said she loved reading my clips/previous articles. So I sent her the following:

Recently I submitted some clips that were well-received, so I'm submitting the following story ideas for your consideration:

12 MEN TELL WHY THEY NEVER CALLED BACK
The date was great, he said he'd call again, and the phone never rang. Millions of women wonder and worry as to the reasons why. These men explain all the different reasons that keep them from picking up the phone. Some will surprise you. Many reasons don't even have anything to do with the date itself.

IS HE CHEATING ON YOU? — Ten Telltale Signs. Ways to figure out if your man is seeing other women would be followed by what you can do to remedy the situation.

Your body and mind are in the best shape they've ever been in. But between your busy schedule, and just not meeting anyone new, sleeping alone has become your state of affairs. STAYING SANE WHILE CELIBATE would be anecdotes and advice from women and men who have been celibate for months and years, as well as doctors, psychologists, and psychotherapists.

THE BEST BREAK-UP I EVER HAD would be a roundup of healthy experiences and ways to achieve relationship closure that help you heal and move on. This would include real-life anecdotes and advice from psychologists and therapists.

Anyone could see what was on my mind by the story ideas I was pitching. I pressed send and took a shower. After drying my hair and putting on a new pair of yoga pants, I went back to my computer. Email from Jessica:

Today's a new caravan for open houses. Love for you to join me.

Hmm, what do you learn on caravans for open houses? The downturn in the economy created an abundance of short sales. How could my readers of women's magazines benefit from that? If I learned more about real estate, staging homes for sale, décor, mortgages, short sales, and foreclosures, I could expand the subject matter I was also growing tired of writing about, as well as pitch to a new group of well-paying publications. I called Jessica, and agreed to join her.

Changing my clothes to look more like a broker going on a caravan, I took my larger purse and grabbed a notebook so I could learn more and increase my knowledge of home selling, buying, and everything in between.

Jessica and I spent the afternoon driving from house to house. I learned about flooring, inset lighting, bonus rooms, and school districts. And, I got to see Jessica in action — confident, detail-oriented, and poised to immediately find the key selling points of every home we explored. Loving her smarts, we ended the day at El Coyote. Over margaritas and burritos, we recapped the day's events and how this fit in with the week's activities of being a successful real estate broker, especially in this difficult market. I was feeling giddy with knowledge, and not ready for the day to end.

"Jess, do you have anywhere to be?" I asked, not sure what I was up for. "I was thinking about taking a walk through the Beverly Center, maybe some retail therapy. I've learned so much today. The best way for me to process information is to digest it at a makeup counter. Maybe Bloomingdale's or Sephora?" I inquired.

"Sure, why not?" she responded eagerly.

We giggled through Sephora, trying on lipsticks, eye shadows, rubbing skin lotions on each other's hands with the zeal of high school girls. The ease and comfort I felt being near her, able to touch and laugh unselfconsciously filled me with joy.

"I never did anything like this with my last girlfriend," Jessica remarked, while inspecting under eye concealers.

"What did you two enjoy together?" I asked, hoping to learn more about her.

"We spent a lot of time visiting each other's parents. Dinner on Friday nights with hers, Sunday brunches with mine. I guess she really wanted a domesticated life. I didn't realize how straight she wanted to be."

"What do you mean?" I inquired.

"She left me for a man. Saw him behind my back while we lived together." Yow, that smarted. I wiped lipstick number five from my mouth and tried to change the subject. "Seen anything here you want?" I said, pointing to the lipsticks.

"Just you, babe." She nuzzled me, made her selection, and walked to the register.

After we each bought a lipstick (mine was mad mauve, hers was peaches n' cream) we went back to the car. As soon as we'd each closed our door, we looked at one another. Before we could buckle into our seatbelts, we started making out.

Twenty minutes later, when the lip-lock cooled down, Jessica said, "Want to go somewhere else?"

"Sure!" I said, bubbling with anticipation, not even caring where it was, as long as it was with her, feeling deliriously happy and joyfully sane. Then Jessica drove to our next destination…

28. Self-Pleasure Shopping

Feeling revitalized, I relished being with Jessica; she was quite intriguing, sexually and otherwise, because she kept so much inside, revealing her secrets slowly and discreetly like a Renaissance courtesan or geisha. I assumed she was a wise, knowledgeable lover who after ending her last relationship was looking to have her love life jump-started, like a car with a bad battery. I longed to tease out and provoke her inner vixen.

I was surprised and pleased when she drove to The Pleasure Chest, a store that sold erotic paraphernalia. Located on Santa Monica Boulevard, between Boys Town in West Hollywood and the newly immigrated Ukrainian community, the parking lot was almost full. There was one spot near the door. Jessica's car slid into the spot.

The store was as packed as a mall two days before Christmas. None of the patrons paid attention to us, two old broads strolling through the aisles of the sexual supermarket. We passed dildos, cock rings, spikes, and leather gear. We each discreetly pointed at items we found ridiculous or horrifying, like electronic-powered penis pumps or dildos longer than umbilical cords.

"With stuff like this, guys need us like they need a third testicle," said Jessica. "Pierced, tattooed, or otherwise."

We turned a corner and faced a floor-to-ceiling wall of vibrators. We stopped and carefully touched and explored each cylindrical pleasure toy, reading the promises on the packages: ribbed, waterproof, soft, pliable, powerful.

"Are you buying anything?" I asked, eager to learn her dildo preferences, thinking this would give me a clue about her sexual preferences.

"Oh, of course," she said.

"Which call out to you?" I asked.

"Simple and uncomplicated is always best," she said, suddenly cool and certain.

Most of the vibrators had a scary, space-age, intimidating mystique. About eight models of waterproof, exotic novelties, all endorsed by a television sexpert from the show *Talk Sex with Sue Johnson*, were at eye level on the wall. We'd both seen Sue's show on the Oxygen network. She was a retired nurse — and about 70 years old. On her call-in show, she spoke about sex with the same delight and matter-of-factness as Martha Stewart preparing a pie crust. So, counting on her expertise, we narrowed our sights to Sue-approved toys.

I took one off the wall, showed it to Jessica, and asked, "What do you think?"

"Good width, not pliable enough. It'll be too hard," she replied authoritatively.

I felt like Goldilocks in the dildo store: too big, too little, or just right? I put it back and reached for another. "What about this one?"

Jessica shook her head. "No, I had one like that. It set off the metal detector in the airport. I was detained and searched," she stated matter-of-factly as she reached for a package containing a sea green item with a purposefully rounded head. It was a cross between the inside of a tube of toothpaste and the sea creature, Cecil, from the cartoon of my childhood, *Beany and Cecil*. It was called *Royal Servant* and the shape resembled the penis of my college boyfriend.

I took the package from Jessica, inspected further, and read the box. It was a keeper. She took another *Royal Servant* from the wall.

"We're buying identical vibrators?" I asked her, intrigued by her dildo confidence and familiarity.

Jessica shrugged. "Years ago, I worked in a store like this in Miami. The police busted the store. I got arrested for lewd and lascivious behavior," Jessica said, laughing, as we each held our purchases and walked to the cash register.

I paused, looked her up and down, and said, "How come I never knew this?"

"I was a different woman in another life. Once your free bird tastes fear, you never fly the way you used to." When Jessica was profound and off-handed, I knew it meant, 'Don't ask any more questions.'

The checkout girl opened each package and inserted batteries to make sure that "he" worked. Then she asked if we wanted to buy the batteries. We each said *"No,"* confident that we had a stash in our respective junk drawers at home. Then the girl asked us, "Please test that the texture and movement is agreeable to you." She was like a sommelier in a restaurant uncorking a bottle of wine.

"He" passed the test and we grabbed our respective black plastic bags containing our *Royal Servant* and drove to my house. Because we each had challenging work days the following day, we shared a friendly hug goodnight before Jessica drove home.

I went upstairs, unlocked my door, and rushed straight to my battery stash. There were batteries there: C batteries, D batteries, and AAA batteries — but no AAs for my new vibrator. Oh, no. I bolted into the bedroom and pirated my television remote. More AAAs. Even now, when I thought my orgasm was within my battery-operated control, self-pleasure was fraught with frustration. The moment was laughably disappointing, like most of my sex life.

The following day, I bought new batteries, brought them home, and tried my new *Royal Servant*. As I rubbed it against my pleasure zones, I felt myself tingling in harmony with the vibrator's hum. I looked at the shape and thought again of my college boyfriend. I laughed because I was experiencing greater pleasure than I did years ago in his twin-size dorm bed, fumbling and sneaking around. I was reminded again that orgasms with men could be over-rated. I could feel this any time I wanted — all this pleasure — at my control — and no one had to buy anyone dinner. Could it get any better?

29. COOL: The Future?

There must be other women out in the world going through sexual confusion and identity awakenings as I was, but where would I find them? I searched the Internet and found a group called the Community of Older Lesbians (COOL) that met near my house. The website stated that the group was for lesbian women age 50 and older. Well, I'd been 50 for five minutes and a lesbian for four, so I guessed I qualified.

Jessica, in support of my sexual evolution, agreed to accompany me, so we entered the room at the community center on the grounds of Plummer Park, off Santa Monica Boulevard. We were faced with a dozen lesbians closer to my mother's age than our own. Some looked like they'd entered a Gertrude Stein look-alike contest. Others had feisty, ageless personalities. One white-haired woman attended with her home health aide. I wondered, "Was her aide a lesbian, too?"

Mary, the meeting leader, 64 and overweight, had a girlish, vibrant spirit and beamed as she told the story of her 10-year anniversary with her partner, Aida. Aida was the 72-year-old braless, grey-haired woman sitting next to me. She gushed about the secluded cabin in Napa Valley where they hot-tubbed, sipped Cabernet, and celebrated their life together.

Hearing Mary talk about her contentment and happiness, I reflected on my mother's last 15 years of life. She was alone, reading books, seldom going out, waiting for something or someone while remaining removed and closed off. How much fuller her life could have been if she'd embraced a Mary or an Aida.

Looking around the room at my possible future, most of the women seemed engaging and happy. The meeting evolved into a discussion about the aging process.

"I don't take long walks the way I used to," said Doris from the back of the room.

Another woman, Gloria, chimed in, "I've had grab bars installed in the showers of my home."

Carmen, an older Latina lesbian, said, "I remember a lecture on aging last month. Someone stood, held their hand up, pointed their index finger in the air, and slowly showed it curling downward, saying, 'This is aging.'" Everyone laughed. My first thought was that Carmen's finger simulated an old man's dwindling, impotent penis.

She said, "Everything just curls up, shrinks, and gets slower."

Everyone nodded sadly. I continued thinking about an old man's penis.

"If you lose something, try to focus and retrace your steps. If you still can't find it, look in the fridge. That's where I find my keys or eyeglasses," said Aida.

"I'm on medication now for anxiety because I worry about little things more and more each year. But I drive better than I can walk," added another.

My favorite part of the discussion was when Mary mentioned that she and Aida went to the same doctors.

"We've told our doctors our sexual orientation," Mary smiled. "We were leaving his office last week, talking about our visit. Two women in the elevator asked, 'Are you sisters?' We shook our heads 'no.' 'Mother and daughter?' 'No. We're lovers!'"

Her comments reframed my thinking that older women were forgettable and uninteresting. If given a choice between Gertrude Stein and Winston Churchill, I'd pick Gertie. She was a lively conversationalist — and she did have those brownies.

So much for a support group, I thought to myself. I had hoped to see someone here my age, a contemporary, for support and encouragement. But then again, Jessica was by my side. So maybe everything I was looking for by coming here, I'd had before I walked in the door.

After my years in the heterosexual world, was this moment even about Jessica? Or was it that I finally felt comfortable being attracted to a woman? The meeting soothed my angst about intimacy with women. There just may be hope for me yet!

Next, Jessica and I went to the supermarket to get ingredients for tomorrow's dinner. Shopping for dildos or dinner was a joyous, experience with her.

In the grocery store, I smiled all the way through the frozen foods, delighted to feel comfortable being attracted — and attractive — to a woman. Later that day, when I was putting my groceries away, Beth called, eager to meet for coffee. We sat at an outdoor table on the top floor of Barnes and Noble at The Grove.

"Remember how guilty I felt that I had a perfect husband who let me do whatever I wanted? Well, Jeff's not perfect — far from it."

"Is he seeing someone?" I enquired.

"That would be too obvious, simple, and average-guy easy. Jeff's quietly complex." Sipping her latte, Beth's eyes searched for the farthest spot in the sky.

"What's he up to?"

Beth chewed her fingernail before speaking, "He has an addictive personality that's gotten us $300,000 in debt."

"What?" I shot back. "That's an avalanche of debt. How is that possible?"

"Twenty five pairs of Italian shoes!"

"Good taste."

"He bought them in Italy, when I was at my Lavender Visions weekend," Beth said, incredulous.

"What did he say about it all?"

"When I stopped screaming at him? He said, 'You have the other side of your life; I have mine. I don't judge you.'"

"So he felt entitled?" I asked, watching Beth's shoulders tensing.

Beth shook her head "Yes." Her eyes welled with tears. I held her as her shoulders quivered, and her tears turned to sobs. In this moment, her life spinning out of control, the luster and allure of being a married lesbian drained away, like her son's college funds had. She wiped her eyes and regained her strength.

"There's more — he spent most of the money on cocaine."

"Is he still using?"

"No. But I'm going to Al Anon meetings and Debtors Anonymous." Beth chewed her nails again. "I wake up in the middle of the night seething with anger. He has a sickness. We'll work to heal him and make him well."

"Other women would get a divorce," I offered.

"Divorce is not an option. We agreed on that years ago. Murder looks attractive," Beth said smiling, on the verge of a laugh or a tear.

"This puts a damper on your dating?"

"Who has time, going to 12-step meetings?" Beth said, now giggling.

"So now you're married to his debts too?" "That's another thing. I filed for legal separation."

I was confused. "I thought you're not getting a divorce."

"It's to protect our assets and not damage my credit. Just legal paperwork."

"I can't believe you're not fighting mad."

"I asked him to move out. But he gave me a sad, puppy dog look and said he had nowhere to go, and no money. He slept in the basement a few nights."

"And now?" I was trying to be supportive. But I was fascinated by Jeff's crazy behavior, hanging on Beth's every word. I always thought Jeff was so down-to-earth. And Beth was the one careening one way, then another.

"We're taking everything a day at a time," she responded more calmly. "One day at a time. I cut up his credit cards. We cook dinner together most evenings. We're working hard to be normal."

"Normal?"

"Balanced," Beth said softly, exhaling, as if telling me her challenges lightened her burden.

I remembered that balanced was one of Jessica's favorite words. Older women are COOL and have a supportive community. Older men are complicated. Still reeling from Beth's hellish experiences, I wondered if anyone really ever knew anyone else.

30. Love Means Never Having to Say You're Sorry
♛ ♛ ♛

Rick, my Facebook friend from an advertising agency job I had a decade ago, posted on his news feed that he'd made very spicy chili for dinner last night...so spicy, he was afraid to rub his eyes.

I dubbed those sharings of minute information pervasive on Facebook to be Narci-posure.

I checked Derrick's page. He posted new photos just yesterday. Since we'd last seen each other about two weeks ago, he'd grown a mustache, gone to his daughter's swim meets (they were darling) and started cross training and preparing for running in a marathon. I was delighted he was keeping busy and not thinking about me.

As I was clicking away from his Facebook page, he instant messaged me for a Facebook chat.

Missing you. Was thinking of visiting. Busy this weekend?

Things were going so well with Jessica. I really wanted to focus on her. But Derrick was still in the picture. What to do? I stepped away from my computer and strode to the kitchen for a Weight Watcher's ice cream sandwich. One of my favorite oxymorons, surely by the time I'd unwrapped and devoured the quasi-tasty, pseudo-satisfying, low-cal treat I'd know what to say to him. I took three bites, then opened a diet cherry Coke to wash it down. Finished every bite. Licked a dribble of vanilla from the wrapper, then crumpled it and tossed it into the garbage. Still no answer for Derrick. Went back to the fridge, pulled out another. They're half the calories of a regular ice cream sandwich, so I wasn't in dangerous territory — yet. Repeated exact steps of previous ice cream sandwich.

Derrick: Don't race over, but if work brings you to town it would be nice to see you.

Nice? I hate that word. It's so blah and adequate. Was I thinking it would be blah and adequate to see Derrick? I should see him one more time, to be certain that we were just a Facebook fling. *Just a Facebook fling?* Was that an article I could pitch? Sometimes I think I'm such a self-help article whore. I couldn't write the article till I knew/lived the whole story — meaning — when I saw him I'd need to end the relationship.

Meanwhile, I was running late for a mani-pedi appointment. I'd check my email later and see how Derrick responded and proceed from there.

Two hours later, my fingers and toes were glistening with *Cherries in the Snow* polish, followed by a visit to Coffee Bean and Tea Leaf on Third Street and La Cienega for a lite latte. After going to my mailbox to pick up *Vogue, Netflix,* and junk mail/discount coupons from the hearing aid store down the street (the average age of people in my neighborhood was Jurassic and deaf), I tossed my keys on the counter and reluctantly checked my email.

Derrick wrote: *I have multiple meetings in L.A. I'll be renting a car, so I can drive and meet you rather than having you be my chauffeur.*

I appreciated Derrick's company. But I was falling in love with Jessica. This "thing" with Derrick was not a relationship…it was a working-through of past hurts and unfulfilled fantasies, sort of a therapy fuck-a-thon with room service and frequent flier miles. In my past, I was so used to men acting attentive and interested while looking over my shoulder at someone else, younger, prettier, chestier — the woman they would talk to after they were bored or done with me. But here was someone who was willing to drop everything and get on a plane to be with me. Wait, a man who desired me. I hadn't really experienced that for most of my adult life. I'd finally gotten a taste of the heady combo of passion and yearning, coupled with caring and tenderness, while being held tightly, lovingly, in a man's strong arms. I savored the thought of our time together. In spite of all that, it really had to end…this trip? The next?

Since Derrick rented a car for this trip, I thought it a good idea for him to pick me up. We'd go to a restaurant in my neighborhood, and there in a public place I'd end it and then walk home. The writer in me wrote it like a scene from a movie, thinking through every detail.

Then I saw his face and the bouquet of flowers he gave to me. Friday night, Derrick was beaming. I hugged him, and he smelled like warm cinnamon rolls.

We went for sushi, five blocks from my place. I ordered a bottle of shoju, a lot like sake only more potent. Shoju warms the palate and goes down easy. Plus, it's an aphrodisiac. That was my first stupid move.

During dinner, I waited for a moment in the conversation that would be THE moment when I would jump in and cut the cord. But like the scared, ungainly girl who could never find her way to jump in, even while playing jump rope, I watched and listened, ate and drank, and never jumped in.

Relaxed and inebriated, I invited him back to my apartment. If this was our last time together, let's make it memorable. Second stupid move. Sitting on the couch, we kissed gently. His graceful, delicate fingers caressed my face.

The shoju kicked in. I took on the libido of a frenzied lap dancer, climbing on top of him for a passionate kiss, my knees pushing into the couch pillows, my crotch flirting with his pelvis. My man-hunger had overtaken me. Derrick was stunned, elated, and gently caressed my behind to guide my rhythmic thrusting. Next, he pulled my hair, bit my neck, and grabbed my ass fiercely. Kissing, humping, moaning and breathless, as we both slid to the floor and clumsily removed our shirts. He lay me down on my back, putting a pillow behind my head. Then he covered my breasts with sweet kisses, not rushed tugs like I remembered from TC's urgency. Derrick made tender love to me. I switched positions with him and kissed his chest.

Pants were being unzipped. I suggested we move to the bedroom. We hopped to the bed. His boxers and my string bikini quickly disappeared as though we'd performed some magical sleight of hand. An hour passed as we kissed, groped, caressed, and aroused each other. Time for the big moment — penetration. So turned on to be naked with a strong man, and be caressing his large cock, I gasped with anticipation, skin tingling with eagerness to feel him inside me.

Derrick was hard! My wetness rubbed up against him. Then he lost his erection. "What? No, not now!" said the voice in my head. I roused the fallen soldier with my mouth, and he was ready again. I positioned myself for entry. We moved together to become one — and we were — for almost 10 seconds. In the dark, I saw he was mortified.

"I'm very excited to be with you. I need some time. Let's sleep on it and try later," he said kissing my cheek. I turned on my side to be cradled in his arms — wide awake, energized, and frustrated.

This had never happened with Derrick before. I'd forgotten that the care and maintenance of a male ego and their erection sometimes takes lots of work and energy — like babysitting someone else's grandchildren.

In the morning I rolled over, opened my eyes, and saw Derrick admiring me like I was the Mona Lisa. Smiling at him, I stroked his face. I kissed his cheek and eased my body up to him, arms wrapped around his neck.

As we continued kissing, his morning erection greeted me. I hoped it would have energy and staying power. Still smooching, I positioned myself to welcome him inside me. Our eyes locked as we both marveled at the moment of easy penetration and glorious sensations. No sooner than we realized our bodies were one, the synchronizing faded, moment gone. Derrick's disappointment set in.

He offered to take me out for a hearty breakfast of bacon and eggs. Not much eye contact as we ate in near silence. Now was not the moment to jump in and end it. All these weeks, I appreciated his attention and flirtation. That part did light me up — the way Diana had described it. I also experienced her feelings about the scintillation of youth. As much as I'd heard men talk about it, and thought so much less of them for it, I was now fully aware of how when youthful sensibilities and abilities were lacking, they tugged at my senses, killing and burying lust. I knew that this was not a love connection, more of a fulfillment of lifelong longings finally consummated.

By the end of our breakfast, when he planted a thin-lipped kiss on my mouth, I was relieved he didn't want more. A swift hug and peck ended the morning as we walked in separate directions, each mumbling a promise to call.

I thought Derrick and I were done, our relationship had run its course, and I didn't have to give my "let's end this" monologue. Relieved, I went home, certain that my future was with Jessica. In this moment I realized that I chose her. I was ready to love her and be a good partner.

I went home, ripped the sheets off of my bed, and threw them into the laundry, eager to wash away my guilt and stupidity for thinking I'd even consider a last tumble with Derrick.

Back at my computer I sent off the following pitch to an editor I'd been working quite closely with lately:

Susan was attending a meeting of her weekly women's support group. That night, the theme was secrets. Each woman was asked to tell a secret they had never told before. Eight of the 10 women shared the fact that they'd had an affair with a woman at one time in their lives.

WOMEN LOVING WOMEN....STRAIGHT WOMEN SHARE THEIR SECRETS would be a round-up of anecdotes told by married, divorced, and single women who have at one time or another had an affair with another woman. Was the other woman gay or straight? Was it a one-night stand? Did they do it to please a man? Did they do it because a man had hurt them? These and other questions would be explored as well as female affairs in history and quotes from noted psychologists and therapists.

This article would be relevant for COSMO because in the November issue the article "Being a Gay Woman" appeared in your magazine. Since the majority of your readers are heterosexual women, I think my article might be closer to home for them.

I called Jessica and left a message: *Missing you, would love to see you.* But I knew that weekends were her busiest time of the week for open houses and new clients.

On Monday, Derrick called me, desperation in his voice. "I need to see you; can you meet me in the valley? Right over the hill near Laurel Canyon?"

I didn't really want to go, but I felt I owed him closure. So I agreed to meet for coffee, midday. I positioned myself at the back table of Starbucks in Studio City, on the corner of Vantage Avenue, with a direct view of the door, casually reading *Elle* magazine while I waited. Three pages into "Hot New Handbags", I noticed him enter, walking towards me.

He sat down in the wooden chair facing me, gazing into my eyes piercingly and with purpose, as if to punctuate the joyousness of his delight. His facial expression said, "She's a pretty one. How lucky am I?"

His eyes continued to focus on mine, unwavering, seemingly unaware of our surroundings or the young, scantily clad actresses lining up for lattes inches away from our electrically charged optic lock.

"My day got a whole lot better the minute I sat down here."

As I glanced up at his piercing, elated eyes, I felt myself begin to glow.

"Don't you want to get a coffee first, Derrick?"

"No, I'm good. I just had to see you."

When Derrick looked at me, with caring eyes, he made me feel decades younger. He's such a loving soul, maybe my picker was broken and I was wrong. Was this man my answer and I was too clueless to see? Would his presence in my life be big enough to stop my wondering? Maybe the issue all along was not men or women, but finding the right person to make me feel loved, all the time. It was a heady moment. I sipped my mocha ice blended, stirring the ice, searching for more liquid, breaking his gaze, so I wouldn't be swallowed up as his eyes continued to drink me in.

During our conversation, he said "safe" and "dysfunction" frequently; no doubt remnants from therapy sessions following the dissolution of his marriage.

"I have something really important to tell you," he said, purposefully. "Our time together has been magical; we both know that. I can never forget a minute of it. But the other night's limp soldier is proof that magic can't last. No matter what happened with us, my life is in Chicago."

"I know that," I responded calmly.

"Being with you gave me the courage to see myself as a new man. Our time together prompted me to get into cross training. I'm in this group with 15 others, including a web designer named Anita. She and I have gone to dinner, but haven't slept together, yet. I really like her. I think when you and I were together the other night, I was thinking about her. I could never...two women...you know what I mean?"

I sighed deeply, knowing all too well what he meant. I did not feel rejected, but instead, gently released. It was a warm, positive feeling.

"Let's go," I said, standing, gently ushering him out the door.

Standing on the street corner, I kissed his cheek. He held me closer. Derrick smelled really good, like hot apple pie on a rainy night. I stroked his face, feeling drenched in hope, of new beginnings for both of us. Grateful for the time we'd spent together. His shoulders and arms were endless, wrapping around me, strong, cocooning me from the world. We both knew this was our last moment this close. As I kissed his cheek again, he tilted his head, so his lips could touch mine. They were big, sweet lips, enveloping. And time stood still in the middle of midday on bustling Ventura Boulevard. Then we were officially making out, as time passed and we were magnetized, smooching it up, one last time, for any passerby to see.

I heard a car's brakes screech, as if trying to avoid a crash.

"Back to work," I said, breaking the lip lock, which felt like it could last an hour longer unless I took charge. We walked in opposite directions to our cars.

I was now ready to move forward, devoting myself to building a relationship with Jessica, certain of smooth sailing given our harmonious personalities.

When I arrived home there were five missed messages, all hang-ups on my voice-mail. I explored further — all from Jessica. I went to my email, nothing from her. On Facebook I had two new friends. Meanwhile, Derrick posted this on my wall:

Thank you for these last few weekends together, some of the best times of my life.

"Shit!" I screamed out loud, realizing he'd posted it for all of my 266 Facebook friends to see…including Jessica! I deleted his comment, and realized why Jessica might not have wanted to leave a message. I raced to the fridge for a diet Coke.

My doorbell rang. I took a long swig of soda before answering it.

"Jessica," I said smiling, while opening the door, trying to act like nothing was wrong. "How are you?"

"Who are you, is more like it," she raged at me. "I was almost in a car accident. I was driving along Ventura Boulevard on my way to show a house, and I saw a woman who looked like MY girlfriend, standing on a street corner swallowing the tongue of some guy. I was so stunned by what I saw, I almost rear ended another car. Luckily my BMW has great brakes. That screech could have shattered glass. Then I go home and learn from Facebook, not from you, that some guy, probably the same guy, thanked you for wonderful weekends! Which weekends were you with him, if you were with me the last few? Or were you?"

"I can explain," I said, clumsily and weakly.

"While you're making excuses, that night you emailed me that you were out "researching" yes, you said researching…is that your word for being a cocksucker!" she yelled, ready to strangle me.

"I love you. I've finally learned that. I was going to tell you tonight. You are the most important person in my life, in my world. I just want to make you happy," I said calmly, slowly, trying to ease the moment.

"You're dishonest, duplicitous, and cheating with men. That's the worst part. You know how I feel about women who flip-flop. You're a pseudo rug muncher on holiday from dick," she blurted angrily.

"I want to be with you…it's over. He's gone, back to Chicago."

"Honesty and fidelity are the foundation of a relationship," Jessica said, calming down, wiping a tear. In this moment I remembered when we first met, she'd been crying — her last relationship had just ended.

"Yes, I agree," I said tenderly, trying to wipe her tear. She pushed my hand away.

"Without honesty and fidelity we were never building anything," she said with conviction. "There's nothing here to talk about. I'm done."

And just like that she walked out the door and slammed it behind her.

"Wait," I screamed opening the door, to run after her. But I knew she was mad and inconsolable.

Storming back into the house, I stomped around, first to the refrigerator, opening the door, staring inside, and then slamming the door. I was so ready to be with Jessica, now I've lost her? Just hours ago I had the attention and affection of two people. I have no one to blame but myself. This is a horrible feeling. I need a bath.

After a half hour of soaking in hot water, I called Beth but got her voicemail. Help, I needed consolation and strategy — so I frantically dialed Julia. The phone rang and rang. I got her voicemail too. Just as I started leaving a message, she picked up.

"I am so glad that you're there," I barked in emotional overdrive.

"What's up? How do you have the time to call me?"

"I went from being the apex in a glorious love triangle to being a turd," I remarked remorsefully.

"What happened?" her voice was soothing, comforting, and immensely curious.

"My Facebook page betrayed me!"

"Let me sign on and see…"

"I deleted it, but for two hours all of my friends could see Derrick's posting on my wall thanking me for these last few weekends."

"That's nice," said Julia. "What's the problem?"

"Jessica saw it."

"Ew, that's bad."

"She saw it after seeing me standing on a street corner kissing him goodbye."

"You're kidding me. Public displays of affection are a no-no," she instructed.

"I know that now."

"What will you do?"

"Luckily my apartment is currently a Haagen Dazs-free zone. Talking to you is helping ease the sting of dual rejection in the same day. I was loved and adored."

"Yes, you were, and rightly so."

"Thanks. Now I'm alone. I should see it as a wake-up call."

"To do what?" Julia asked, with the calm and authority of a therapist.

"When the old me used to fall down rejected, I'd pick myself up and get online, to a dating site, shop for someone, and go out and date, with a burning intensity to fill the empty void that was newly created, with another live, though usually inappropriate life form. But for the first time, I don't want to meet someone new. I want Jessica. Only Jessica. Being with someone now is about being with her, not just another live body."

"I'm proud of you. That sounds like progress and maturity."

"She'll never speak to me again."

"But you're so charming."

"She caught me with a <u>man</u>, and thinks I'm a flip-flopper. She called me a cocksucker."

"Them's angry words. True lesbians don't like when their girls shop around — especially in dickville. Now you know what fiercely loyal looks like."

"I'm ready to be loyal," I fired back.

"That's not who she saw kissing a man on the street."

"Ew, the way you say it, it really sounds disgusting," I responded, groaning.

"She needs time. You need time," Julia advised.

"I love Jessica. I need to <u>win</u> her back," I said with certainty.

"Win? Love is not a lottery ticket."

"I will <u>work</u> to get her back," I said, hopeful.

31. Help Me to Help Myself and Help You Too

To keep my mind off of dating, relating, and obsessing about Jessica, I dove into my work like it was an Olympic swimming pool and I was an Olympiad in training. I used this time to write and problem-solve simultaneously.

I started by writing a series of pieces under the heading, *Are You Ready for a New Relationship?*

The first article began: *Are you looking for a new love too soon after splitting with an old one?* I used my angst to get to my own sane conclusions and pay my rent as well.

There's an old saying that the best way to get over an old love is to find a new one. In reality, nothing could be further from the truth: Experts say that a woman fresh from a breakup shouldn't go on a mad stampede to replace an ex with a new lover.

As part of writing my stories, I interviewed experts: doctors, therapists, and authors of relationship books.

A professor of behavioral sciences said, *"When a relationship ends, it's important not to rush into a new one, but to spend time with yourself in self-evaluation. Develop a sense of your needs; otherwise you run from one mismatched relationship to the next."*

A psychiatric facility treatment leader echoed his sentiments, stating, *"Learning what you want in a relationship isn't easy when you're still reeling from the aftershock of a breakup. Feelings of hurt, anger, disappointment, and intense neediness can cloud your judgment and make you vulnerable to starting — and quickly ending — a string of unsatisfying involvements. That's why you should take a time-out when a relationship ends, giving yourself time to heal, even if you're feeling lonely. It's better than throwing yourself headlong into another relationship."*

Headlong? My middle name is headlong, or is it headstrong? Hello, I'm Headlong Headstrong, the neurotic serial dater. The life span of my relationships is as long as a good haircut. I wish I would've had the good sense to write about this subject months ago — my whole life would have been different — less opera and less pain.

To further focus my life, I went to a yoga class every day. I had about two new friends on Facebook every week. No one really reached out to instant message me or visit me, or leave their current life or wife and have sex with me. Most evenings I took a long walk and then ate a small dinner (as seen in the article I wrote for *Shape* magazine entitled *Move More Eat Less, Just in time for Bikini Season)*. Eating lighter helped me sleep better. I woke up each morning (alone) refreshed, energized to start the day. I turned my introspective urges into being incredibly productive. I believed that helping others would bring me closer to solving my own relationship issues.

I breezed through writing *Transitional Relationships, the perfect medicine to soothe self-esteem:*

It's not realistic to believe that the first person you meet will be the man of your dreams. Don't underestimate the value of a transitional relationship; this type of casual but healthy involvement can do much to prepare you for your next serious relationship. In effect, you can "practice" in a transitional relationship all the things that went wrong in the last one, and feel emotionally ready when the real thing comes along.

One sex therapist said: *The transitional relationship is highly valuable to the emotional mending process, and also gives you the opportunity to explore different types of men. You'll see what you need and want from a man, as well as what you don't. Knowledge may boost your self-esteem. Valuable things can happen that make a person ready for a good, strong relationship.*

All of these experts' insights fueled my articles as well as my personal growth. My relationship series got great feedback and raves. My fees per article were increasing. I was offered a syndicated advice column that appeared in newspapers three days a week and simultaneously on a website. I had now ascended from self-help diva to relationship royalty. Since I was never someone who could take a good thing and accept it without picking it apart, I still wondered: If I was such an expert, where was my relationship?

But I kept my head down and kept writing. A few months later, my friend Rachael, another writer who focused on sexual addiction issues, used excerpts of my work in a women's anthology that made it to the *New York Times* best seller list, and also on a site where people paid per click to read the content.

One day Rachel met me for coffee at Kings Road Café on Beverly Boulevard. We sat outside, each drinking café mochas out of giant white cups. I couldn't get over the gorgeous pair of Grecian sandals she was wearing. "Your shoes are so great; they make your legs look endless. The leather is soft and yummy," I said admiringly.

"Glad you like them. You could get a pair too," she said, while reaching into her purse for a letter-sized envelope. "This is for you."

I opened the envelope and took out a check for 22,000 dollars! I put my hand over my mouth to soften my gasp of delight. "What's this for?"

"Australian rights to the book, U.K., Japan. The blog is taking off too. Women in Europe really clamor for your advice," Rachel exclaimed.

"My angst is a gold mine?" I said smiling, bringing the cup to my lips, sipping and feeling the warm sweet mocha slide down my throat. The only thing that would make this moment more glorious was if I had someone to race home to, to tell my news and good fortune.

Rachel and I said our goodbyes. I strolled home, smiling, wondering who I could call, who I should call. Beth was having marital and money problems, so dialing her would seem like gloating. Diana might ask for a loan. Who would be happy for me and might even benefit from my newfound flash of cash?

32. Big Fat Check
♛ ♛ ♛

What could I do with 22,000 dollars? How should I use that money to change my life? I could deposit it in my account and draw from it when I needed help paying my rent. That's a sensible, conservative woman's approach to money. That won't make me happy or change my life. But it will keep me safe. Wasn't it me who really valued being safe and sane just a few months ago? What happened to that, Sara? She gambled on two lovers and crapped out.

I held the check in my hand, feeling it could burn a hole in my skin. I couldn't bring it to the bank till I spoke to someone, shared my news, and explored possibilities. I felt overjoyed and invincible. This was my lucky day! I picked up the phone and dialed Jessica. The phone rang four times. She picked up. Her hello sounded hesitant.

"Jessica, it's Sara, calling you as a potential client. I might be in the market for a condo," I blurted. Before I could think about what I'd said, and how stupid it was, she put me on hold. I used this time to figure out what I'd say next. My mind was blank.

"Sara?" she said, clicking back to me. "My three o'clock for tomorrow just canceled."

"Meet me for coffee at three tomorrow," I insisted. "I know you're free now."

"It would help if I knew what you were looking for?" she asked, in a highly professional demeanor.

"Looking for?" I said tentatively, knowing that what I really wanted was her, in my life again.

"What size condo, amenities, gym, terrace, pool?"

"I don't need a pool," I answered, feeling stunned to be having *this* conversation.

"Your price range is under a half million… or more?"

"Oh, under, definitely," I said, realizing she was serious and only focusing on the work aspects. I didn't want to piss her off…again.

She paused, and then with an ounce of reluctance said, "Okay. How about meeting near Bob's Doughnuts at Farmers Market?"

"Deal. Bob's Doughnuts, three p.m. See you tomorrow." I hung up the phone and danced around. Then I prepped the tub for a luxurious bubble bath. I needed to soak and rehearse what I'd say.

The next day at 2:30, final preparations: good hair, clear face, looking good, not too excited. Who am I kidding? After trying on four or five different shirts and finding the one I liked, I spilled coffee, which created an obvious stain the size of a baby's fist, right near the left boob on my favorite blue blouse. After changing that shirt and triple checking that the right buttons were in their designated holes, I turned to walk out the door. Hand on door knob, the phone rang. An editor was checking on my progress for an article due next week.

"Uh-huh, uh-huh, talk to you later, uh-huh, good, can we--uh-huh, talk later? I'll call you back? Bye."

Finally, out the door, walking two blocks to *The Grove* to meet Jessica, I heard the screech of two ambulances, followed by a police car. They're all heading where I'm going! Walking another two blocks I realized I'm walking towards the scene of a three-car collision. Glancing over to make sure none were Jessica's BMW, I kept walking, heart pounding, in anticipation of our meeting.

Meanwhile, the sounds of sirens are replaced by the rustling of a leaf on a tree mere inches from my head. Looking up, I realized I'd just dodged a shoulder full of bird poop. Glad it happened near me and not ON me, I smiled, feeling lucky. Walking south on Fairfax Boulevard, I felt encouraged by it being a warm, sunny day in February. The closer I got to Farmers Market, the faster my heart beat. If these aren't loving, yearning feelings, I don't know what is.

Farmers Market: chattering crowds of people, talking, laughing, eating different kinds of food. Senior citizens pushing baby carriages. Walking, looking, hoping — there she is — there's Jessica. Should I hug her? Just a friendly smile? I'll let her lead the way. Jessica smiled and leaned into me, not quite a hug, almost like a body peck. Her hair smelled as great as I'd remembered. I tried not to swoon.

"Hey, how are ya?" she said, more officious than warm, pulling a clipboard and pen out of her purse.

"Coffee? Anything?" I was trying to push the social angle of the meeting.

"Um, uh, soy latte?" she said tentatively, as she made herself comfortable at a table with folding chairs.

I obediently searched the nearby coffee sellers for a soy latte, not easily found in this part of the market. But I knew it would make her happy, so I went to the far end of the market. I brought back chocolate cookies too.

"Is everything all right?" Jessica asked, concerned I'd been gone a while.

"Fine. Great," I said. "They have the coffee you like on the other side…and these too." I presented the cookies.

"Thank you. I pulled some comps for condos in this neighborhood as a starting point for what you'd be looking for."

"How's your coffee?" I asked, easing the conversation to being friendlier.

Jessica sipped, and went back to her clipboard. "Look at these and tell me what you think."

"I trust you'll find great places."

"What's your down?" she asked off-handedly.

"Down?"

"Down payment, your deposit."

I offered proudly, "Work has been going great. I'm syndicated and a big hit in Europe. I just got a check for 22,000 dollars."

"That's nice, Sara, congratulations. But how much can you put down to buy a place?" she said officiously, growing impatient.

"Twenty-two," I restated, proudly.

"You brought me all the way here for 22,000 dollars …anything else you can add to that? You should know you can't buy a hot dog stand in this town for that kind of money." She gathered her things as if ready to leave.

I grabbed her arm. "Don't go. Listen to me."

"I wish you respected me enough to not waste my time," she said coldly.

"With my writing and your real estate smarts we could create a real estate column together. I'd quote you the way I quote shrinks and therapists. This would increase your visibility, build client recognition, revenues — yours and mine. We'd pool our resources; we could make enough money to buy a house with a pool."

"You're an adorable dreamer, Sara. But I live on planet earth," she said curtly.

"Hear me out," I mustered, not knowing where I was going. "I'm seeing this as a business opportunity that could benefit both of us. You teach me more about real estate; now that I'm syndicated, your point of view could be all over the country. Articles on: How to help women hold onto their homes, or buy foreclosures before auction. I could help you become the Suze Orman of real estate."

We each paused and looked into our coffee cups, both surprised by what I'd said, and the potential of it all.

"You talk a good game," she said, still not looking at me.

"I'm not playing. I'm for real. All these months away from you, I was thinking about this moment, and what I could offer you…if it would be good enough — compelling — if I would be good enough. I've grown into a better woman — more mature and responsible."

"Who sleeps with men," she said, insistently.

"When we first met, you said there was so much you wanted to learn from me. I want to learn from you. Remember that Pet Shop Boys song, *I've got the brains, you've got the looks, let's make lots of money.*"

Jessica laughed. "You were always fun to be with."

"Work with me. Teach me about short sales, for example. We can work on articles together; down the road, maybe a book. Buying a short sale for the long haul."

Jessica looked up and focused on me. "I'm listening. Continue."

"See me from a business point of view. Let me show you the potential."

"And then what?" she asked.

"Be open to anything possible."

Our eyes met, both smiling. In this moment, I was drenched in hope.

33. Dream On...It Takes Two
♛ ♛ ♛

I knew if I won Jessica's trust I'd have to work hard to keep it and build on it. I immersed myself in learning everything I possibly could about the buying, selling, and maintaining of real estate.

I pitched stories about the homes and lifestyles of the women I wrote self-help articles for. I got to know a slew of new editors from design magazines such as *Elle Décor, Metropolitan Home,* and *Dwell.* Stories like *Spruce Up Your Studio Apartment, Living Large on Less,* and *Ten Steps to Refinancing Without Tears,* all sold easily and effortlessly. They also paid better than some of the other publications I'd been writing for.

Meanwhile, Jessica and I were spending a lot of time together working on story ideas, sharing dinners at night, looking at houses and condos on weekends. At first, we worked together as friends, and then, one night our work life melted… into a romance.

We were at my place, outlining an article about *How to Start a Vegetable Garden, Even on Your Terrace.* Jessica was uber-serious. I tried to be playful. We ordered mushroom and garlic pizza. I opened a bottle of red wine. We ate and drank.

The pizza was very salty, so we drank some more. On the couch laughing, she reached past me to refill her glass. Her arm grazed my leg. The clean scent of her magnificent mane was intoxicating. I leaned in for a cheek graze that became a smooch. Yes, it was that same couch where I'd had my last night with a man, my infamous misstep with Derrick. I thought how I needed to burn that couch, to silence the stories it could tell. Or maybe that couch was my passport to erotic adventures! That night was incredibly passionate, as Jessica and I both unleashed our wild girls, moaning and groaning each with fierce feline moves and frenetic energy. It was clear to both of us that neither had been intimate with anyone since our break-up. I think that made her receptive to trusting me, again. I saw this night as a small victory. But I knew that battle was not totally won.

After that, work nights ended with affection, sex, and pillow talk before falling asleep. Our professional goals of building greater magazine visibility and real estate expertise were coupled with growing as a romantic team. But two people collaborating get growing pains. We certainly had our share. I like to be comfortable when I write. Jessica saw this as me dressing sloppily, with dirty hair and a ripped shirt.

Jessica was repulsed, "Pigpen, stink bomb. Smellier than a man. "That's a low blow."

"You know how, better than I do," Jessica fired back.

"Will you ever forget? Will you ever let go and trust my love for you?"

Another day, another argument, same subject. She thought I was a slob who couldn't wash a glass properly.

"Oh no, you don't call this clean?" I remarked sarcastically, examining the stained drinking glass. Then I dropped it on the floor, so it would break. "Now it's not a dirty glass…its garbage — I'll clean it up, 'cause I'm a planner."

"I don't think I can work with you," said Jessica.

"Me either," I admitted. "But I can't imagine life without you… So I'll do better."

That evening we went out to dinner. I was clean, dressed up, and well-coifed. Jessica was all smiles, attentive, and quite turned on in the restaurant. After dinner we stopped off at a supermarket to get some fruit for breakfast.

While I was in the produce aisle a man approached me. Seems he recognized me from my photo in the *Toluca Times*. We spoke for a few minutes. Jessica watched from a distance. She saw him touch my shoulder and give me his card.

"Who was that?" she inquired, with more than a hint of jealousy.

"No one."

"No one gave you a business card?" she continued, amping up her rage.

"He reads the column, wants me to write about drywall and mention him, 'cause he's a drywaller," I explained, hoping this would calm her.

"You think he's attractive?"

"He wants me to grow his business, not suck his dick. Is that all you see whenever I talk to a man?"

"I trust you. But you're an attractive woman. I don't trust men."

"Your jealousy can get bigger than a house."

"Good we have sleepovers rather than a mortgage," she snapped.

We carried the groceries and went home in silence. Once we started unbagging our purchases, a heat came over both of us. We turned, touched, kissed, caressed, and ended up making love on the kitchen floor.

After a few months of going back and forth between our apartments with overnight bags, we each decided to give the other a drawer and some closet space. So now it felt like we lived together — at her place during the week, and mine on weekends.

One Friday night, I was standing in my kitchen, at the cutting board, slicing red and green peppers for a stir-fry. Early Joni Mitchell songs were wafting through the air.

I felt a gentle hand encircle my waist as warm lips kissed my neck. It was Jessica, offering me a glass of red wine. We each sipped from our goblet, locked eyes, and nodded to one another, a pleased expression. After many months together, we had learned each other so well; we needed few words to say, "Yes, this wine is good."

She stirred the onions in the wok, and then extended her arm to me, indicating I should bring the peppers. I marched my red and green slivers to the stove. She tossed and stirred them. The peppers seemed to dance in the wok, sizzling.

Jessica put down her wooden spoon and reached for me. As we kissed, I felt my open heart pressing against hers. A deliciously warm feeling cascaded from my head to my toes. The feeling was not from a hot flash or the hot kitchen. It was from the wonderfulness of being loved and accepted and loving back.

My life was so much fuller and more joyous once Jessica became a part of it. I finally appreciated and savored the intimacy we shared. We moved together in the kitchen or working on story ideas, or on vacations like a fine Swiss watch: caring, helping, and ticking forward; getting things done and delighting in the journey. Dinner at home, barefooted, was never so delicious.

Midlife was smarter. I knew how happy I was because I measured it against decades of disappointment, despair, and aloneness. This moment may not have looked like the life, or love, or partner I thought I'd have at this point in my life. I was glad I was able to be open and accepting to embrace a happiness I never thought was possible.

After about nine months and 20 articles themed about real estate for women, Beth suggested turning them into chapters for a self-help real estate book. *Women Can Own Foreclosures* practically wrote itself. The book was an easy sell too. Using public relations ingenuity we were able to get mortgage companies to offer it to prospective clients. Jessica and I appeared on *The Ellen DeGeneres Show*. We teased Ellen that she'd owned more than a dozen homes, but none were foreclosures. Our book took off!

We were able to parlay the success of our first book into a second: *Women Owning Real Estate, the Workbook*. This featured tables and worksheets that helped women prepare for mortgage meetings. It also included encouraging quotes and motivational exercises with space for journaling.

We did a book tour, with question-and-answer seminars. This was thrilling because after months of being huddled over our computer, we were out in the world visiting bookstores in large cities where smart women lined up to buy our books, hear what we had to say and share success stories. It was exhilarating to hear their experiences of feeling empowered, negotiating with lenders, doing things they never thought they'd do, and the freedom and confidence of owning their own homes. We were creating value while building credibility for ourselves.

Then one day, in the bookstore in my neighborhood, the most gratifying thing happened. We were setting up for a Q&A presentation at the *Barnes & Noble* at *The Grove*, just off Fairfax. It was a huge store with about a dozen little cluster points where you could spend the day reading and exploring. The entire place was crowded. Fifteen minutes before the event was supposed to begin, people were filling the event area.

As Jessica was carrying an extra box of books to the signing area, she walked past the biographies section. A man stopped her, eyed her up and down, and began flirting with her. Jessica smiled and appeared interested. Putting the books down, she began talking to him, like she had time to spare.

Frantically I searched the floor for her, eager to set up the books, anxious about the day's presentation. Seeing her and recognizing him, all fit, fine, and white-haired, my adrenaline was pumping at double speed. With the confidence of a superhero, I approached him. "Hi, remember me?"

Ack said, "No."

I was enraged, "You don't remember me? I'll show you something you'll never forget!"

I kissed Jessica deeply and passionately, dipping her back in a long, swooning romantic moment. In front of everyone, I felt all of our mutual jealousies melting away and gloriously happy with my choice of partner. To Ack I blurted, "The next time you kick someone out of bed without fucking them, remember that." To Jessica I said, "Come on, doll. We've got books to sign."

I took her hand and we sauntered up to the table where a long line of eager book holders awaited our signatures. Before picking up our pens, we grabbed each other's asses affectionately and smiled at one another.

When the second book was published, we received a big advance. This coupled with Jessica's relationships with all of the listings services and mortgage brokers enabled us to live the dream we'd encouraged others to do. We bought a house together — a little pink cottage in Toluca Lake. We got a great price because it was part of an estate sale. It had a big back yard and a pool.

So without obsessing about the lack in my life I was able to move from magazine writing to books, increase my income, and find love with a delightful life partner. Packing and moving seemed easier. The things I'd been collecting, saving, and hoarding when I lived alone had finally lost their luster. There were more boxes for the trash than the moving van. With less baggage of all kinds, my new life was leaner and smarter.

Our first night in the house, I luxuriated in the tub. Now I was a homeowner, with Jacuzzi bubbles. Another dream had come true! While soaking, I reflected on who I was, and who I'd be now, living in this house.

I realized, love and sex are ideally a package deal. In my life I hoped sex would bring love. But the outcome was usually life-threatening, disastrous, or just plain loveless. Growing loving feelings and building intimacy seemed like a greater challenge and a more necessary goal as I got older.

I'd finally relinquished my quest for men. I gave the pursuit one last attempt and found it disappointing and painfully trying. Was I a lesbian by birth or sexual orientation? Not quite. But I preferred the company and intimacy of women at this point in my life because women over 50 are better companions than men. They know how to do things well, in and out of sexual situations. They know what they like and aren't afraid to express themselves (in and out of bed). They have hair on their heads, hope in their hearts, and a timely pedicure.

I believe that many women and most of my friends who never married (straight or gay) evolved into the husbands they were raised to marry — unclogging sinks, refinancing mortgages, and earning incomes that provide for a small family. They developed into full human beings rather than Barbie dolls waiting for their Ken doll to complete them. (I don't think married women are Barbie dolls, but many of my generation were raised to think they were deficient without a partner.) Where are those versatile, dynamic women this very minute? They're home re-wallpapering their kitchen or attending a book club with friends.

Attention must be paid to my invisible demographic! I want *Playboy* magazine to have a monthly feature, "boomer babes", rather than a steady diet of bleached blond mammary Amazons, fresh from their cheerleading days, devoid of facial expressions, pubic hair, or library cards. I feel validated and encouraged that mid-life women anchor the evening news, telling America what's happening in the world. America's favorite talk show hosts were mid-life women: Oprah was unmarried, rumored to be in the company of women, yet she vehemently denied it. She earned millions more than any man and wielded greater power and influence than most successful corporate giants. Then there's our new pal, daytime's darling, Ellen DeGeneres, a publicly acknowledged lesbian, with the approval of habitual audience member, her own mother Betty. If everyone's world could be so loving and accepting, life would be a lot easier.

My late mother wanted me to be happy with someone who loved me. I may not be the woman she raised me to be, but the world had changed rapidly since her youth, and with even greater velocity since my own girlhood.

If I had less than a half century left, it was my experience that the men I met were elusive, inadequate, and rejecting. Climbing the penis tree became a pointless hike of disappointment on a crumbing branch of dead wood. After much reflection and deliberation, my smart choices were to be alone or with a woman.

I'd unlocked my heart to someone who opened their arms to me, eager to build and share a life filled with affection and mutual respect. It just happened to be a woman. As a young bride, was I a lesbian in training? Growing and changing is a giant part of leading a healthy life. Repeating the same mistakes (with men, yeah, them again) was self-defeating and tiresome. I had to remind myself of that quite often.

But what about sex — with a woman? When my eyes were closed and I was in the dark and someone was pleasuring me — in that moment did it really matter if they were a stranger or familiar, a man or a woman? Feeling good was downright pleasurable and rare. Many graduates of the "free love" generation spent lots of time not putting love and sex together, sort of fucking a la carte, and then marrying whomever they woke up with the moment they realized they should be married. My ex-husband did that. Very little was personalized in my marriage, other than the monogrammed towels.

I was eager for this new chapter in my life. Susan Sontag said, "Do stuff. Be clenched, curious. Not waiting for inspiration's shove or society's kiss on your forehead. It's all about paying attention. Attention is vitality. It connects you with others. It makes you eager. Stay eager."

Toweling off, still exhilarated by my new environs, I realized that the house, the book, and my birthday all happened around the same time. I'd dreaded birthdays in the past, but somehow this year it wasn't about getting older, but instead about new beginnings, brighter opportunities, and better days.

Jessica said she planned a housewarming/ book party. Maybe a birthday cake would be thrown in for good measure. I trusted that whatever she'd arrange, it would be better than being hijacked to an intervention. She knew how to soothe my anxieties.

34. Little Pink House
♛♛♛

Scrubbing up my best party face and attitude, I slipped on a silky black and white floral cocktail dress, backless and hemmed just below the knee. As I lined my eyes and lips, I realized I was having a good hair day. How wonderful to celebrate my birthday at a time when my faith in love had been revitalized — with hope.

By the time I was out of the bathroom, Diana had arrived, eager to greet everyone. "All hail your loveliness," I said, kissing her cheek.

"Get yourself a champagne," she said. "And get another for me. Hostessing is thirsty work. You know I'm not a fan of women together, but I could see you two will last forever," Diana said, as we clinked glasses.

The doorbell rang. I moved to the front door and opened it.

"Julia!" My eyes brightened as we kissed each other's cheek. "How are you?"

"Full of news! You won't believe what's been happening" she gushed.

"I haven't seen you in weeks. With you it could be anything."

"Oh, it's something really great. Your head will explode with surprise."

"Hit me with surprise," I offered.

"I was trolling through Craigslist for end tables, and then found myself searching in my usual places."

"You mean people finding?"

"You know me. The next thing I knew, I met Harv and Cleo. Harv was in the music business. Cleo is a retired flight attendant. They listed as a couple in search of a companion. And they found one — me."

"That's very nice," I said, "Sounds like you had a good weekend."

"That weekend became a life-changing experience." Julia put her arm around me, laughing. I don't have to pick a team. I've been selected — by a couple — with a big house in Sonoma. I'll have my own room and a run of their vineyard. You'll have to visit sometime."

"What?" I asked, incredulous.

"I'm moving to Sonoma the end of the month!"

"To service Cleo and Harv? Together, separately, or while stomping grapes?"

"I see your brain exploding," she said, giggling. "I'll be overseeing the print marketing for their vineyard and tasting rooms. Sometimes I'll be with Harv, other times Cleo, or the three of us together. I'll have a job, feel wanted, and not be alone."

While I visualized the physical logistics of all this, I found myself saying, "So you'll be in a trio and have a job?"

Julia high-fived me. "And I'll have health insurance. The perfect trifecta."

As Julia moved to the bar to get a drink, Beth tapped my shoulder. We hugged.

"How are you? Is Jeff parking the car?"

"I'm sorry to spring this on you. I couldn't bring myself to call and tell you. He's home, packing, moving out," she said, looking down sadly. "Our boys will both be in college in the fall. It's a good time to move on."

I was sorry to see my friend so blue. I touched her shoulder.

"Change and moving on lead to good things." Looking me in the eye, her tone changed. "So I 'm here stag today," she said, eyes darting around the room.

"Speaking of moving, I'll tell you something to spin your mind in another direction. Julia's leaving town. She'll be living with a couple!"

Beth's eyes widened. "Get out of town, really? Good for her. Does Diana know?"

"Have you seen Lila?" I asked.

"Her car was right behind mine. Wait until *you* see Lila." Beth offered.

I glanced over my shoulder, and there was Lila, regal, and very close to her was another woman. The two gave each other a knowing glance. The younger woman, Janna was tall, with thick, shoulder-length amber hair framing her face with a fringe of bangs. She touched Lila's shoulder and held her cane while helping remove her jacket.

As I strode towards Lila, she smiled at me. "Happy birthday, dear. Congratulations on the house! Do you remember Julia and I talked about the marketing class we took? Janna was our teacher."

"Glad Julia invited you, Janna," I said.

"Julia didn't invite her. She came with me, cookie."

"That's nice. You two have become friends?" I said, surprised.

"More than," Janna said, shaking my hand.

"You and Janna spent time together since class?" I asked Lila.

Janna chimed in, "A lot of time. She's getting all A's, or should I say O's." Grinning mischievously, she kissed Lila's cheek and then walked to the bar.

Lila looked at me, beaming. "I'm taking a page from Beth's book. Keep up your yoga, Sara, it pays to be flexible. And I have you to thank."

"Me? I don't understand."

"When you were seeing April, I saw that a really great part of you was shining through. You made it safe for me. I got to see someone I knew be in a different kind of relationship and find happiness. So that's what I'm trying to do."

"Oh? Oh! I'm glad. I envy her. I've wondered what it would be like to kiss you."

Lila stepped closer to me. She put her index finger to my lips, saying, "Hold that thought. I'm delighted you considered it in the first place. I adore you, always have."

A wave of warmth surged through me. Looking around I saw my dear friends, drinking and laughing in my new home. I exhaled, feeling joy and contentment.

When I overheard Janna talking to Lila, the two looked into each other's eyes. To see Lila look so engaged in the moment, happier than I'd seen her in years, was a great gift to me. They walked holding hands, peaceful; confirming to me that women were great companions for other women, not a consolation prize for male disappointment.

Strolling in the opposite direction, I spotted Beth. "Did you talk to Lila?" I said.

"And her new *friend*, Janna?" Beth chuckled, knowingly. "It happens to the best of us...I'm waiting for it to happen to the rest of us."

As we both walked towards the bright light, Jessica wheeled out the cake while everyone sang. Enthralled by Jessica's illuminated face, my heart was full.

I mumbled a wish for myself, "I wish to stay happy." I gazed around the room at the group of bright gals, confident, loving their lives — this was a club I'd recently become a member of — and delighted to be here. I glanced at Julia, Lila, Beth, and Diana. We all loved each other. But marriage or partnership was a different kind of love. Lila might be on the brink of that; Beth was disengaging from it.

In this moment, my answer became clear! I had something I'd searched and researched for in my life and in my work — love — with someone who was my best friend, who knew and accepted me and made my heart sing. I'd found someone to laugh me out of bad moods with silliness, to trust, who can cope with the "for better or for worse" challenges of the

AARP years. And she'd made this big party today, and wheeled out a giant birthday cake — because she loved me. I saw her smile behind the bonfire of candles on the cake. As everyone sang happy birthday, love flowed through the house and through me. I blew out the candles, and they re-lighted. To me this was a sign that I'd gotten a second chance in life, at happiness. This was my first birthday as my new self. It took more than half a century, but I like me and my life now.

Finally, the candles were blown out. Jessica cut the cake. She stuffed the first piece into my mouth, the way a bride does to a groom at a wedding.

Diana walked to the side of the pool with her camera, for a clearer view of me and Jessica arm-in-arm. The fact that Diana wanted to take this photo meant to me that she'd finally accepted my life with a woman.

Then Diana fell into the pool. Others took off shoes, jackets, and jumped in too.

Julia caught my eye and cocked her head for me to join in. I shook my head no.

Friends jumped into the pool, laughing, and eating cake, all carefree celebrants. I was reluctant to jump in and join the crowd. Beth and I looked at each other, hesitant.

Diana swam in front of me and said, "Sara, this is the best party ever. I'll remember this day the rest of my life!"

"Me too!" I thought, joyously, still watching the others, averse to jump in, more of a reporter than a participant.

"Any more wine?" said Diana. "Where's the corkSCREW? I love that word."

"It's Sara's birthday! Pop the champagne!" Lila insisted.

Jessica passed out glasses to everyone, who rallied in a semi-circle, as Beth popped the cork and filled everyone's glasses.

"To the happiest of birthdays," Jessica gushed, raising her glass. "To Sara, my best girl. Her writing, tenacious ways, and big dreams have brought us to this day."

Beth added, "And this great house. May you be happy here together."

"Thank you all. You've known how to surprise me, overwhelm me, happy-end me, and leave me speechless," I said, eyes welling up with tears of happiness. "A toast to my best girls! You are my love, my family, my everything. I may have forgotten to have children, but I was smart enough to have all of you in my life." As I reached for Jessica, she put her arm around me, held me closer, and kissed me firmly on the mouth. Exhilarated by the day, "You, holding me is the greatest birthday gift."

"I hope you're happy," she said, joking. "Clean-up tomorrow will be a bitch."

Arm-in-arm, gazing at the splashing and water hijinks of friends frolicking in the pool in their party clothes, like children, I said to her, "What a rowdy bunch of old broads." We laughed, hugged, and kissed again.

During my breathless sprint through 341 blind dates, a gnawing hunger ravaged my sensibilities and self-worth. I'd had enough blind dates to last all of the lifetimes of all of the people in that pool. Now with an abundance of love in my life, my plate was full and my hunger satisfied. I had no idea that the best part of my life would begin after 50.

What do you call a **50-**year-old woman who buys a 40-count box of tampons?

An optimist.

What do you call a **60-**year-old woman who buys a 40-count box of tampons?

A woman who takes good care of her younger lesbian lover.

What do you call me?

A woman with a bendy body, flexible attitude, and a truckload of hope — enough to last the next half century.

The day after the party, back to work, I dashed off a short piece about relationships for one of my self-help editors. The article practically wrote itself:

Diving Into a Relationship Head First — Have You Found the One?

How do you know if you've met the person you feel confident about spending the rest of your life with? That's a question and answer that lives deep inside of you. But here's some helpful points to ponder:

As you look into the future, do you see your love there, sharing similar life goals? You both want a business together, travel, same point of view regarding family and children?

Can you two talk for hours without being bored, having good communication and sharing common interests? Conversely, can you be quiet together, experience the silence without being bored, comfortable in knowing that good silence can be better than good conversation?

For you, "I have never loved like this before," is not a clichéd song verse; it's how you really feel. Do you miss each other when not together? Did you trust each other immediately, and feel safe with them? Can you make each other laugh? Are you warmed by their voice and smile? Like each other's friends? Do you want to be together all the time? If most of the above are applicable to you, stop reading an article about how to be in a great relationship. Go and enjoy.

CPSIA information can be obtained at www.ICGtesting.com
Printed in the USA
BVOW071846130513

320609BV00001B/27/P